CLARKE

DECEMBER 2013 - ISSUE 87

FICTION

NON-FICTION

Neil Clarke: Publisher/Editor-in-Chief
Sean Wallace: Editor
Kate Baker: Non-Fiction Editor/Podcast Director
Gardner Dozois: Reprint Editor

Clarkesworld Magazine (ISSN: 1937-7843) • Issue 87 • December 2013

Daedalum, the Devil's Wheel

E. LILY YU

Sit down, sit. You'll hurt yourself jumping around like that. No, don't shout. Quiet studio on a quiet night—a rare thing. Why ruin it?

Come from? Difficult question. I was there in the city of Sharh-e-Sukhteh when a potter glazed his bowl with a leaping goat. I was there when Ting Huan painted animals onto his paper zoetropes and set them slinking and lunging in the hot air from his lamp. I am in the twenty-fourth of a second between frames, where human perception fails. Right now, in fact, I'm shining on theater screens and on the glass of cathode-ray sets and in the liquid crystals of monitors across the world. And I'm here with you, because you called.

You didn't? Usually my votary burns his arms against the lightbox, or dies over and over in a spare room where he can film himself taking an imaginary bullet to the chest, applying what he observes—ah. That scrape, where your head hit the corner of your desk. That would have been enough.

Naturally you'd fall asleep over your work. It's one a.m. and you've been pulling eighty-hour weeks for as long as you can remember. Production deadlines, yes. No shame in that.

Can't help, sorry. That's your job. But lean your head against my shoulder. I'm sympathetic. I'll listen.

What, the whiskers bother you? The beach-ball skull? The fangs? The tail? I thought you'd appreciate the potential for infinite stretch and squash. I'll smooth them all out. How's this?

Frogfaced is an unkind way of putting it. You didn't have those objections to Maryanne, and she approximates the classic pair of stacked spheres.

Very simple. I can see right through you. You're like a cel pegged under glass. Your four affairs. Your ten-year marriage, eroded by your devotion

1

to me—I appreciate the compliment, by the way—and meanwhile Isabelle swelling, suspecting, expecting. Your lust for attention that leads you into other women's arms. Your streak of mulishness. You're a con man. A cheat. A shyster. A magician. I like you.

Not Him, no, but I'm the closest you'll get to the quickening of life. Triacetate and clay and cats using their tails for canes. I'm on the other side of reality, the better side, where physics is like lipstick, dabbed on if needed, and there's no such thing as death. It's all in the splitting of the seconds, see.

Twenty-four frames every second, or the illusion stutters. Belief flickers and shatters. Even if they splice the ends together, the soundtrack will veer off. So I'm demanding, when it comes to sacrifices and offerings. At least 86,000 drawings for a feature film in two dimensions. In three, your weary flick, flick, flick through a dumbshow of polygons and nurbs, tweaking and torquing.

Speaking of offerings. Open your mouth for me. Wider, or it'll cut you. Stop squirming. It's only 35mm. There.

My left eye will do for lens and light. My right hand will be the takeup reel. Keep your chin up.

Here's your life projected on the wall. Your parents in crayon, and there's you—watching Looney Tunes in your pajamas, drawing penguins in the margins of your homework. It runs in your family. Your father loved Felix, and your grandfather snuck into nickelodeons on Saturdays. I'll crank faster through the litany of school, except those stretches where you were scribbling pterodactyls and fish. There's—what's her name?—gone. Alice. Beth. Chenelle. Danielle. She liked your cats, at least until you started drawing them with howitzers.

Please stop moving, you're making the picture shake. The faster I wind it out of you, the sooner this'll be over.

Art school. Elizabeth and Farah, tall and short, marvelous until they found out about each other. Your classes in anatomy, visual effects, life drawing, character rigging. What a crude and clumsy portfolio. But here's the job offer, finally. Here's your two dirty, grueling years as an assistant. Here's the second offer, the promotion, the raise. Now the wedding suit and blown-over chairs on the seaside. The late nights modeling and posing doe-eyed animals. The fights with Isabelle. Plates crashing to the floor. Cracking. Team meetings, sweat darkening an inch of your collar, making long wings under your arms. Your manager telling you how much your work stinks, how much he'd like to take your ideas into a cornfield and shoot them, how close you are to the edge of the axe.

2

That's it, the reel's run out. Feeling better? I thought so. Good to have it out, the fumes tend to build up explosively. Now—

Ah. I thought you'd never ask.

These are the standard packages:

A. Your work will spring to life. It will dance, it will convince, it will enchant. Your transfer of mocap to wireframe will never seem dull or mechanical. Your hollow shells will breathe and blink and blush. It will look like voodoo.

You're interested, I can tell. Oh, easy. The accelerating pulse of color in your cheeks. Besides, I can guess. Thirty-six years old, overlooked, unknown, a failing marriage, a father-to-be. Success is survival.

The price for all of this? Merely—long, sleepless nights with me. Nine thousand of them. And your wrists. You have such lovely, supple wrists. I shall mount them in mahogany, I think. What do you say?

Of course, that's only sensible. I'd want to know, too.

B. is a rise. Not meteoric, but assured. Lead animator, then director of animation five years later. Doesn't that sound nice? That's not all. Shortly afterwards, you become head of the studio, or you split off to form your own profitable company. The less expensive option, this.

Expensive? You'd make oodles off of it! You'd be famous! Admired! Fawned over! Only gradually would you notice, as you floated up like a birthday balloon, how far you always were from your pen and tablet. The animated films you produce, your name splashed everywhere, you'll never touch with your own hands. All the work will be done by other people's brushes and pencils and styluses. You'll be so busy with decisions and budgets that you won't have a thought to spare for art, for the boy you were at seven, doodling flip books at the kitchen table. So.

No? Not satisfied? Neither of these appeal to you? A true artist! You have talent. I can see that. You want to press your fingerprints into history.

Well then. I offer you hunger. A mastery of my arts and an inextinguishable desire to do things better and differently. Break the box. Upset the game.

Others? Of course. Charles-Emile Reynaud. William Friese-Greene. Méliès. Yes, all of them. Yes.

Why, nothing at all. Not a clipping from your fingernail. Not a red cent.

I am quite serious.

An intelligent question. Only if you stand still. Only if you stop innovating. Take Reynaud, for example, smashing his praxinoscope as the more fashionable cinématographe swept Paris. Friese-Greene dying with the price of a cinema ticket in his pocket, which was all the money he had. One shilling and tenpence. The others—them too. You must not stand still. My hunger is a painted wolf that will chase you around the whirling rim of the world. Run, spin the wheel, and life will pour from your fingers. Geometry and time will be your dogs. Hesitate, let the bowl turn without you, and—snap! you are mine.

That was a joke. You are one of mine and always were. The question is, do I like you better at your desk, or do I prefer your median nerve coiled delicately on a cracker with caviar to taste?

Ha! That was also a joke! Why flinch? You used to appreciate the soft, surreal psychosis of cartoons. Mallets and violence! Bacchanals, decapitations, shotguns, dynamite! That's my sense of humor.

I don't give, darling. I take. Sometimes I negotiate. It's always unfair.

Choose. Don't make me wait, or you'll wake up with stabbing pains in your arms and claws for hands. A slow dissolve on your career. No love, no money, no lasting memory.

Begging doesn't suit you. Your heart's transparent to me. I don't give a pixel more than you do for your family. Your Isabelle would be only too happy—but to the point. Our transaction.

They can't hear you from here.

Certain privileges come with being a monarch of time and a master in the persistence of vision. I am nothing in the security cameras. Not a shiver. Not a blot.

Are you sure? A kiss, then, to seal the bargain. I'll peel this little yellow light out of you. You won't be needing it.

A gift I gave you, once. No matter. Tonight your department head will dream of you and what you could become. Expect a meeting next week.

You might. But you'll have the odor of vinegar to remember me by. From the decay of acetate film.

No, I would never think of calling you a coward.

Of Alternate Adventures and Memory

ROCHITA LOENEN-RUIZ

Adventure Boy was twelve when he met Mechanic for the first time. They had gone to an exhibit celebrating the removal of the barrier between Central City and Metal Town. He remembered feeling proud. His mom, after all, had played a key role in building bridges between the two worlds and if not for her efforts, the barrier would still be there.

"There's someone I want to introduce you to," his mother said.

He'd registered the peak in her voice that could mean excitement or trepidation, but before he could feel anything himself, they were being welcomed into a circle of metal men.

"This must be your son," someone said. "I'm very pleased to meet you. I hear you're quite the Adventure Boy."

A hand was extended to him, and he looked up. Light glinted off Mechanic's domed head and Adventure Boy picked up the static threaded through his voice. An unrelenting old-timer, he'd thought.

"Well," Mechanic said. "won't you shake my hand? I assure you, shaking hands with me won't turn you into a metal can."

It was the hidden taunt that prompted him to reach out and clasp Mechanic's hand in his. He noted the temperature of metal against his skin, but where he'd expected cold, Mechanic's hand was warm. "I may be old," Mechanic said, "but I'm still upgradeable."

The other metal men laughed and Adventure Boy registered signals of relief from his mother.

"I'm pleased to meet you, sir," Adventure Boy said. He didn't know what else to say because he'd never heard of Mechanic and he didn't know why his mother felt it was important for this man to like him.

After that introduction, his mother was summoned by Central City's governor and Adventure Boy was left to wander the exhibit on his own.

Here were replicas of a life he'd never known. Photographs and reliquaries that meant nothing at all to him. They were part of his mother's long ago life, not his. He had come to awareness in Central City, and he only knew this place with its smooth asphalt, ordered subdivisions and neatly manicured front lawns.

The photographs made him wonder though. He stared at captured images of piles of rusted metal, disembodied machines, and deserted buildings and he couldn't help but wonder what it had been like when his mother still lived there.

"You should visit it someday," a voice said behind him.

It was Mechanic. His hands neatly folded behind his back, his eyes directed at the replica of a building called the Remembrance Monument.

"Of course, the streets are silent now," Mechanic said. "We're being integrated into Central City's workforce and there's no need to maintain the workshops and the shelters. It's a foolish fancy that none of us are allowed, but if you stand directly under the Remembrance Monument, you can still hear the whisper of voices from those who've gone before."

"Why would I want to do that?" Adventure Boy asked. "I don't belong there at all."

Mechanic inclined his head. His face was blank, in the way metal men's faces were blank. But Adventure Boy couldn't help feeling as if he'd hurt the metal man somehow.

"I mean, I was born here," Adventure Boy said. "I'm a citizen of this place. Also, Metal Town is no more, so . . . "

His voice trailed off as Mechanic stepped away.

"You're right," Mechanic said. "This is your city. I hope you enjoy the exhibit. It was good to meet you, Adventure Boy."

As he watched Mechanic walk away, he couldn't help but feel as if he'd done a great wrong.

An alternate child will be a good addition to your home. Memomach industries works to create the perfect child to suit your needs.
—Memomach Industry ad—

He remembered the time he was refused a place on the school softball team. He listened to the soft-voiced principal as she tried to explain it to him.

Alternates were different. They could run faster. They had more stamina. It wouldn't be fair to the children of the makers.

In time, he learned not to want. He tried to blend in. He was, after all, his mother's child. In his second year at school, another alternate child transferred in. He tried not to speak to the other, and the other did not speak to him. They sat side by side on a bench watching the others play, not speaking a word.

It would have gone on that way if not for another transfer. Unlike them, Jill Slowbloom was noisy. She laughed loud and she made jokes. She was clumsy as well.

"My parents said they wanted the perfect child," she said. "But they meant the perfect child for them."

Her laughter drew them out of their shells. They were no longer two, but three, and when the term ended and another alternate transferred in, they became four.

"We could start our own club," Jill said.

"I'll be point. Eileen will notate. And you and Jeff can follow my lead."

For a while, he felt like he belonged somewhere. Then the new term ended. Jill transferred out. Eileen moved away. He and Jeff were left staring at each other, not knowing how to fill the silence that was left behind.

Perhaps, he thinks. *Perhaps if I go to Metal Town, I will find the words to fill the silence. Perhaps I will understand more.*

Father wears the face of a numbered man. He wears the suit, he carries the briefcase, he drives the car.

At home, he morphs into someone who Mother argues with over their dinner.

"I don't see why you feel the need to indulge him," Mother says.

"Mechanic thinks it will be good for him, and I agree," Father replies.

They are discussing Adventure Boy's desire to visit Metal Town.

Mother doesn't wish them to go, but Father sees no harm in it.

"I don't understand why you want to see that place again," Mother says. "I shudder when I remember how I almost lost you there."

"But you didn't lose me," Father says. "And we can't deny him this. If he wants to know it for himself, then he should know it for himself."

"I won't go," Mother says.

"If you don't want to go, you don't have to go," Father replies.

Adventure Boy lies on his back and stares up at the ceiling. He had bought a picture of the Remembrance Monument and Father had hung it up. At night, the lines of the monument glowed in the dark.

Mechanic's words rang in his ear.

"You can still hear the voices of those who have gone before."

8

Smooth asphalt morphed into rough tarmac and the neatly ordered lawns of suburbia were replaced with fields full of high grass and wild sunflowers with faces turned towards the sky.

Father had rented a tour car; it was decorated with yellow sunflowers and bold black lettering announcing the name of the official tour agency.

They were the only visitors so far. It was a Saturday and most tourists came in after twelve.

Adventure Boy rolled down the window. A light morning breeze caused goosebumps to rise on the surface of his skin. But after that initial contact, his skin warmed and they vanished.

"It's a much smoother ride than I remember," Father said.

Adventure Boy turned to look at him.

Without his suit, Father looked like one of the makers. His face was not as rigid, his shoulders were relaxed and he wore a plain t-shirt and jeans just like all the other fathers Adventure Boy saw at school.

"We've never talked about it," Father said. "But Metal Town is a painful memory for your mother. She came to consciousness here. She loved it and yet she wanted nothing more than to escape it."

"Is this where you two met?" Adventure Boy asked.

Father smiled.

"You could say that," he said.

There was a pause and then Father said, "It was here that I brought her into being."

With the unification of Metal Town and the Central City, Metal Town's dwellers were promptly absorbed into the general work-force. Metal Town soon became redundant.

Proposals for the renovation of Metal Town are ongoing, but until then, it has been kept in its original state for the sake of those who wish to revisit an important part of the reunification history.

—Recorded guide from Metal Town Tours—

"These were my quarters," Father said.

They stopped before a cluster of buildings. Adventure Boy noted the signs of decay on the metal scaffolds that kept the buildings together.

Father stood at the foot of the one of the houses. It was washed in gray, its shutters were wide open and one of them looked out at a field of sunflowers.

"Do you want to go inside?" Father said.

What precautions were carried out to preserve experiments from being stolen or taken away? This house, which holds the tools of a master maker, was secured with a special reader that identified visitors through codes implanted in their optic lenses.
—From Guide to Metal Town—

"It's still here," Father said.

Was that amusement in his voice? Father stooped, and Adventure Boy saw it. A small screen was set into the doorjamb.

"Try it," Father said.

Adventure Boy bent down and pressed his eye to the screen. Nothing moved. The door didn't budge.

"It doesn't work," he said.

"We'll see," Father replied.

He bent down and pressed his eye to the screen. There was a flash of green and a click.

"I can't believe they haven't put that out of commission," Father said.

With a push, the door swung open and Adventure Boy was assailed with the smell of liquid oil, and the essence his mother took once every fourteen days.

"Is this . . . ?"

"Yes," Father said. "Here is where your mother became aware."

The open window looked out on the sunflower fields. He tried to bring up an image of his mother. He remembered the moment when he first came to awareness. He remembered her voice echoing within the confines of the room that became his own.

"He's not waking up." It was a soundbite from the past.

"Be patient," Father's voice. "Waking up takes time. You should know this very well."

"But if I failed . . . "

"You have not failed," Father again.

He'd opened his eyes, and the room came into being. Walls of powdered gray and the smell of oil and essence pervading the air.

Then Mother's face was in his vision.

"You're awake," she said. Relief colored her voice. "Welcome to the world, Adventure Boy."

One of the archived stories is that of an early alternate. Created to be the perfect housewife, this alternate was so designed that it could easily pass as one of the makers.

There is no exact record of her progress.

—Metal Town Tours—

"Were you happy?" he asked.

"She was as I envisioned she would be," Father said. "An alternate girl who was also quite human."

"I know she is as you wanted her to be," Adventure Boy said. "But, were you happy?"

"I am happier now," Father said. "She broke her program, just as she was meant to. She became herself."

Outside was warmer. It was mid-morning. They had been in Metal Town for less than an hour, but to Adventure Boy it was as if he had been there for a lifetime.

They parked the touring car close to the center.

"It's good to walk," Father said.

And like that they walked into the shadow of the Remembrance Monument.

Remember.

A voice whispered through his circuits. He thought of the moment when he met Mechanic, the warm and solid grip of Mechanic's hand and the urgency that rushed through him in that moment.

I want to see.

The thought rushed through him.

He stood there, looking up at the huge monolith that housed the harvested memories from the hundreds of thousands of Metal Town's dwellers.

Urgency flooded him. He wanted to run. He wanted to hide. He wanted to . . .

He blinked and he was surrounded by warmth.

Remember.

Tiny little pinpricks filtered through his consciousness. He was seeing and yet not seeing. The landscape shifted. He was inside of the monument and he was outside of it.

Father's eyes were closed as well. His mouth hanging open as if he were suspended halfway to speech.

He shut his eyes and saw a vision. The tarmac buckled beneath him, the sunflower fields hemmed him about, and behind him was the roar of the Equilibrium Machine. Its bellow shook the air and he trembled. That great maw would consume him, would crush him, would take him down into recycling and a loss of all that he had come to love.

Despair consumed him.

And then she was there.

Mother. Her eyes flashing bright, her voice ringing in the air around him.

When he came back into himself, they were sitting at the foot of the monument. He wasn't at all surprised to see Mechanic speaking with his father.

> *There are consequences for every choice we make. Be sure you understand before you make a decision.*
> *—Mechanic, Words to the Wise, 14th ed. Ilay Press—*

> *Heritage can be a burden. History can be a burden. Everything can be a burden if we choose to make it so.*
> *—Mechanic, Words to the Wise, 14th ed. Ilay Press—*

Mother never asked about their visit.

They came home and they went on as if they had never been to Metal Town. From time to time, he would dream, but he woke before he started crying.

"Back in the day, my memory would be fed to the monument," Mechanic said. "But government has decreed that we can't do that anymore."

"This body grows old," Mechanic continued.

They sat there listening to whispers that they couldn't understand.

"I had to modulate your receptors a bit," Mechanic said. "Your systems would have broken down without intervention."

"Thank you," Adventure Boy said.

Father didn't say anything. He simply sat there, his head cupped in his hands.

"Memory is difficult," Mechanic said. "We all live with the recollection of who we were. Your mother rescued your father. Theirs was an unusual situation. I didn't think they would try to create another exactly like her."

"I'm not like her," Adventure Boy said.

"I know," Mechanic replied.

There was a pause and then the metal man turned to look at him and Adventure Boy could have sworn he smiled.

"You're like me," he said.

The next time he saw Mechanic, it was at the unveiling of the new government's plan for Metal Town's rehabilitation.

He had grown into a new body. This one was taller and broader than his twelve year old one. He was living on his own now, earning a living as a regular Adventure Boy.

"Feeding the dreams of the masses," a voice said behind him.

He looked down into Mechanic's upturned face.

"You may change," Mechanic said. "But I don't forget an imprint."

The governor had come onstage and was giving the usual speech.

"How old are you now?" Adventure Boy asked.

Mechanic cackled before he replied.

"Older than you. Older than your mother. Older than your father. Almost as old as the Monument they want to tear down."

"What?"

"You're an alternate, aren't you?" Mechanic said. "Surely, you're listening to what the governor is saying."

It was true.

"Redundant buildings," the governor was saying.

As if those words were enough of a verdict.

"Relics of a bygone era," the governor continued. "But we must move on. We must move forward."

He could hear cheers coming from makers and alternates alike.

"But what about the memories?" Adventure Boy couldn't help asking.

Mechanic shrugged.

It was all the answer he needed.

We are always unraveling threads as we strive to weave them together. We think we can move towards tomorrow without yesterday. We forget that yesterday gives us the courage for today, and yesterday is the foundation of tomorrow's dream.
—Mechanic to Adventure Boy—

Records show that our model children grow up to become model citizens. These are the kinds of citizens we need as we look towards our joined futures.
—Government statement on the creation of alternate children—

It hadn't been all that difficult to find them. Awkward Jill had turned into a climber. Eileen created metal art. Jeff surprised him most of all. The silent boy played music in a club frequented by metal men.

What was not surprising—they had all sat under the shadow of the Remembrance Monument.

"It's as if it was calling to us," Jill said.

He couldn't keep from staring when a smile bloomed on Jeff's face. It was the first time he'd seen anything like it.

"We're supposed to be model citizens," Eileen said dryly. "Some would say you were planning anarchy."

"It's going to be risky," Adventure Boy said.

"We know," Jill replied. "Don't pay attention to Eileen. It's just how she is."

"If we're found out, there's no telling what they'd do to us," Adventure Boy went on.

"You only live once," Jeff said.

"I don't know if this plan will even work," Adventure Boy added. "And you do know we could all end up being recycled."

"Nothing tried, nothing gained," Eileen replied.

"You guys . . . "

"You're planning something," Father said.

He looked up from the console he was working on.

"It's no big deal," he said.

"Remember what you are meant to be," Father said.

"I'll remember," he replied.

His father's words hid a message.

This is between you and me, it said.

The days were hectic and short. Word was that the government was accepting bids from demolition teams.

"We have to do it soon," Jill said.

No one would suspect them. Four alternates could not shut down the plans of a city. But they had to try.

When Mechanic showed up at his door, he didn't know whether to be angry or thankful or sorry.

"I hear you might be planning something foolish," Mechanic said.

Adventure Boy crossed his arms and stared down at the metal man. When he was twelve, Mechanic had seemed larger than life. He still had substance, but Adventure Boy no longer feared him.

"Are you here to stop me?" he asked.

"Do you want to be stopped?" Mechanic said.

He uncrossed his arms and looked Mechanic straight in the eyes.

"No," he said. "And we won't be stopped."

For every action, there is an equal and opposite reaction.
—Newton's Third Law of Motion—

"My son has plans. I don't know what because he hasn't told me.
But he is also his mother's son."
—Father to Mechanic—

"You are your mother's child," Mechanic said. "She was also fearless even when afraid."

"She has no part in this," Adventure Boy replied.

"But she has," Mechanic said. "Some part of you was born from her memory of Metal Town and the Remembrance Monument."

Adventure Boy shrugged. He had already ensured that his mother would escape any repercussions. Also, she was well-respected and known for her collaboration with the government. Surely, she would survive his actions with little damage to the reputation she'd worked so hard to build up.

"Even she could not foresee this," Mechanic said. "We mold our creations into our idea of what they should be like, but we also give you the ability to break that mold. Your mother is an example of this."

"What do you want?" Adventure Boy demanded.

"Your mother fitted you well, but there are things you have yet to learn," Mechanic said. "Please. Allow me to lend you my strength."

Where are you going? Where do you come from? Where are you
now? Who are you? Who do you know? What do you want to
achieve?
—Life Questions, Guide to Finding your own Path, Mackay
and Manay—

Mechanic lists down names and numbers, formulas, addresses, and contact points.

"Why?" Adventure Boy asks.

"There are things you can do with a small army," Mechanic says. "But there are things you can do better when you spread your net wide."

Adventure Boy has no words to speak his thanks. He watches Mechanic's fingers as they type out messages on different screens. The words change in formulation, but the message is all the same.

I am calling in a favor.
I need your help.
Remember the bonds we share.
Remember.
Remember.
Remember.

Adventure Boy understands what those words mean now. He understands why he cannot allow the erasure of accumulated memory. No matter how insignificant or how unimportant those memories may seem, no matter that Metal Town is deemed obsolete, he can't allow those memories or those dreams to vanish without a trace.

"Here's how we planned to do it," he says to Mechanic.

They huddle around the table, four alternates and a metal man whose time is coming to an end. Beneath their hands, their dream of the future takes shape. Adventure Boy sees it as a network of roads flourishing, Jeff sees it limned in light going on into eternity, Eileen sees it as a fan unfolding again and again and again in limitless space, and Jill sees it as a flower that blossoms and blossoms and blossoms over and over again.

It is the vision they bring to the table—this promise of a future filled with the dreams and the memories of those who have gone before.

There can be no true reconciliation without acceptance. Until we
see both of our worlds as occupying an equal place in history,
unification is an empty word.
—Justice Torero on the unification of Metal Town and
Central City—

When it starts, it is like a droplet of water falling into silent space. No one notices the movement, but slowly it spreads. Here and there, the earth shakes. Memory rises and people start to talk in sentences that start with: *Remember when.*

Memory becomes a living thing.

As the heat of summer washes over Central City and its dwellers swelter in the shade, what started as a small droplet grows bigger and bigger until it takes the shape of a summer storm that rattles the windows and doors and washes away the heat.

In the quiet fragrance that follows, memory blooms and with it the vision of a tomorrow.

Alternate Ambassador Saunders has purchased a parcel of land in Metal Town. She is the first of Central City's recognized citizens to reclaim land in the place where she came to awareness.

Her partner, Nick Wood, has purchased a lot fronting the former garage building, claiming nostalgia and sentimentality.
—Central City News Network—

Folk musician, Karina Melendez, has purchased a parcel of land in what was formerly known as Metal Town. Claiming a desire for peace and a return to the earth, the land is fit for farming. It also boasts an acreage of wild sunflowers.
—Central City News Network—

In a startling new trend, Remembrance Monuments are being established in the first four wards of Central City. Open to Makers and to Alternates alike, the Remembrance Monuments are meant to house memories both personal as well as public.

In the section open to public viewing, memorabilia is displayed that depicts the progress of Makers and Alternates alike. An interactive timeline allows viewers to enter the stream of thought. This kind of exchange is a first in Central City. It is hoped that this endeavor will further interpersonal relationships as well as preserve the history of the times.
—Central City News Network—

"There are no more borders," Alternate Girl says.

She has come to visit Adventure Boy on the eve of reunited Metal Town's inauguration. For the past six months, she has endured a storm of demands. Critics have accused her of everything from being regressive to being senile.

But everywhere, the alternates were rising. They refused to be silenced. They refused to allow Metal Town to be forgotten.

"It's not yet as I would like it to be," Adventure Boy replies.

"Of course, it's not," his mother replies. "If you were so easily satisfied, you would not be my child."

In the silence that falls between them, there is a kinship closer than any Adventure Boy has felt before.

"Why?" he asks. "Why did you make me?"

"Because," she says, "even if I want to forget, someone needs to remember."

He turns to her, and his puzzlement turns to understanding. In the palm of her hand she holds a chip. It has the marks of wear on it, but its casing is still golden.

"You know whose it is," she says. "When I made you, he was also in my thoughts."

Wordless, he takes the chip from her hand.

"When?" he asks. "When did he pass?"

"What passed was his body," Alternate Girl says. "You hold him in your hands."

Even if she doesn't say the words, he can hear them.

He remembers Mechanic telling him that they are alike and he knows this is a gift he cannot deny.

"Will I still be myself?" He asks.

"You will always be yourself," Alternate Girl replies.

He hands her the chip and bends toward her.

"Then," he says. "let this body also house his memory."

The world around him changes. He changes too. Mechanic is a memory. Mechanic is a dream. Mechanic lives on inside him.

He has no regrets.

ABOUT THE AUTHOR

Rochita Loenen-Ruiz is an essayist, fictionist and a poet. A Filipino writer, now living in the Netherlands, she attended Clarion West in 2009 and was a recipient of the Octavia Butler scholarship. At present, she is the secretary of the board for a Filipino women's organization in the Netherlands (Stichting Bayanihan).

In 2013, her short fiction was shortlisted for the BSFA short fiction award. Most recently, her fiction has appeared in *We See a Different Frontier, Mothership: Tales from Afrofuturism and Beyond, What Fates Impose, The End of the Road* anthology, and as part of Redmond Radio's Afrofuturism Event for the Amsterdam Museumnacht at FOAM museum.

Silent Bridge, Pale Cascade
BENJANUN SRIDUANGKAEW

The knife of her consciousness peeling off death in layers: this is how she wakes.

She is General Lunha of Silent Bridge, who fought one war to a draw as a man, and won five more a woman against adversaries who commanded miniature suns.

The knowledge reconstitutes piecemeal in the flexing muscles of her memory, in the gunfire-sear of her thoughts as she opens her eyes to a world of spider lilies skirmishing in flowerbeds, a sky of fractal glass. She is armed: an orchid-blade along one hip, a burst-pistol along the other. She is armored: a helm of black scarabs on her head, a sheath of amber chitin on her limbs and torso. There is no bed for her, no casket enclosing her. She comes to awareness on her feet, at ease but sharp. The way she has always been.

Grass crackles and hisses. She draws the blade, its petals unfurling razor mouths, and recognizes that this weapon is personal to her. All generals have them: a bestiary of blades and a gathering of guns, used to an edge and oiled to a sheen. She maintained a smaller collection than most; this was one she always kept at her side.

The grass is stilled, coils of circuits and muscles and fangs, petroleum stains on Lunha's sword. She fires a shot into its vitals to be certain. A detonation of soundless light.

Her datasphere snaps online. Augmens bring one of the walls into sharp focus, an output panel. At the moment, audio alone.

"We had to make sure you were physically competent." A voice keyed to a register of neutrality, inflection and otherwise; she cannot tell accent, preferred presentation, or much else. "It is our pleasure to welcome you back, General Lunha."

"My connection is restricted. Why is this?"

"There have been some changes to data handling at your tier of command. We'll send you the new protocols shortly. It is routine. You'll want a briefing."

"Yes." Lunha attempts to brute-force access, finds herself without grid privileges that ought to have been hers by right.

"Your loyalty to the Hegemony has never been questioned."

"Thus I've proven," said Lunha, who in life served it for sixty years from cadet to general.

"We will not question it now." The panel shimmers into a tactical map. "This world would offer its riches and might to our enemies. Neutralize it and the woman who lures it away from Hegemonic peace. Peruse her dossier at your leisure."

The traitor planet is Tiansong, the Lake of Bridges, which in life was Lunha's homeworld.

Their leader is Xinjia of Pale Cascade, who in life was Lunha's bride.

Naturally she questions whether she is Lunha, rebuilt from scraps of skin and smears, or a clone injected with Lunha's data. The difference is theoretical beyond clan altars; in practice the two are much the same. There is a family-ghost copy of her floating about in Tiansong's local grid, but that too is a reconstruction from secondary and tertiary sources, no more her soul or self than her career logs.

The grid enters her in a flood, though like all Hegemonic personnel above a certain rank Lunha is partitioned to retain autonomous consciousness. For good measure she runs self-diagnostics, which inform her that she is not embedded with regulators or remote surveillance. Perhaps it is a sign of trust; perhaps the reconstruction is experimental, and the biotechs did not want to risk interfering with her implants. She entertains the thought that she never died—severe injury, a long reconstruction, an edit of her memory to remove the event. The report is sealed, either way.

They've given her a tailored habitat: one section for rest, one for contemplation, one for physical practice. Being in this profession, she has few personal effects; most are accounted for. Not merely equipment but also the keepsakes of conquests. Here the gold-veined skeletons of Grenshal wolves, there the silver-blossom web of live Mahing spiders. A Silent Bridge shrine for the memories of elders, compressed snapshots of their accomplishments, proverbs and wisdom. Lunha did not consult them often, does not consult them now, and examines the altar only to ensure her family-ghost does not number among them.

Her grid access continues to be tight. She may listen in on military broadcasts of all levels when she cares to, but she can't communicate. Public memory is a matter of course and she checks that for civilian perception of Tiansong. To the best of their knowledge Tiansong embroiled itself in civil war, during which a new religion emerged, spearheaded by Xinjia. A dispatch would be sent to return Tiansong to peace.

Reports on classified channels are somewhat different.

Out of habit she evaluates troop strength, positions, resources: this is impersonal, simply the way her mind works. She estimates that with Tiansong's defenses it'd require less than a month to subdue her homeworld with minimal damage. In a situation where that isn't a concern, it would be under a week. Quick strike rather than campaign, and entirely beneath her.

For three days she is left in isolation—no other being shares her space and she lacks social access. The void field around the compound forbids her to step far beyond the garden. On the fourth day, she stirs from meditation to the hum of moth engines, the music of shields flickering out to accommodate arrival. She does not go forth to greet nor move to arm herself; it seems beside the point.

Her handler is purebred Costeya stock, a statuesque neutrois with eyes the color of lunar frost. They wear no uniform, introduce themselves simply as Operative Isren.

"From which division?" Lunha tries to write to Isren, the right of any general to alter the thoughts and memory of lesser officers. She can't.

"Operative," Isren says, and nothing else. They bow to her in the Tiansong manner, hand cupped over fist, before saluting her. "Your situation's unique."

"Why am I required? It is no trouble to flatten Tiansong."

Isren has knelt so they are level; they have a trick of arranging their bearing and their limbs so that the difference in height doesn't intimidate. "A bloodless solution is sought."

"There are other Tiansong personnel in active service."

When Isren smiles there's something of the flirt in the bend of their mouth. "None so brilliant as you. Xinjia of Pale Cascade is a labyrinthine opponent. She has brought awareness of the public sync to her world and had the opportunity to spread the idea before we imposed embargo. She boasts . . . disconnect. In essence she's become an infection."

"Has she achieved it? Disconnect?"

A shard of silence pinched between Isren's professional circumspection and the situation's need for candor. When they do speak it is delicately, around the edge of this balance. "Not through the conventional methods. Her way entails ripping out network nodes and reverse-engineering them. Fifty-fifty chance for cerebral damage. Five to eight thousand have been incapacitated, at last count."

Lunha browses through available reports. Risk of brain death or not, Xinjia has gained traction, so much that she has been made First of Tiansong. It's not unanimous; nearly half the clans posited against her. But nearly half was not half, and Silent Bridge tipped the scale. Her plans have been broadcast to twenty independent worlds. "Removing her won't suffice."

"No. You are invested in keeping Tiansong well, Xinjia alive, and that's why we brought you back."

"Let me travel there. I would assess the situation on the ground."

"That was anticipated," Isren says. "We are on Tiansong."

When Lunha last visited her homeworld she was a man. Among family she's celebrated only as daughter and niece, for all that she flows between the two as water over stone. Whatever her gender, General Lunha's face—pride of several clans—is too well known, and so she puts on a mesh to hollow out her cheeks, broaden her nose, slope out her brow.

She travels light, almost ascetically. One firearm, one blade. Tiansong currency, but not too much. Her one concession to luxury is a disruptor array to guard against targeting and deep scans. Isren does not accompany her in person; on the pristine sea of Tiansong phenotypes, Isren's Costeya face would be an oil slick. The operative has no objection to blending in, but on so short a notice, adjusting musculature, complexion and facial tells is beyond even Isren.

Lunha avoids air transports and their neural checks, keeping to the trains and their serpent-tracks. She takes her time. It is a leave of absence—the idea amuses and she catches herself smiling into the scaled window, her reflection momentarily interrupting art ads. One of them urges her to see a production of *The Pearl Goddess and the Turtle*, done by live actors and performed in a grid-dead auditorium. No recording, no interruptions.

At one clan-hold she says she is a daughter of Razor Garden; at another, in different clothes and with a voice deepened by mods, Lunha introduces himself as a groom newly marrying into Peony Aqueduct. At each Lunha is received with courtesy and invited to evening teas, wedding dinners, autumn feasts. Despite the tension of embargo they are hospitable, but none will so much as breathe Xinjia's name.

Her breakthrough comes while she sits in a kitchen sipping plum tea, legs stretched out and listening to an elderly cook who fancies she resembles his middle son, long lost to a gambling addiction. "You want to destroy a nemesis, you teach their child to gamble," the cook is saying as he spoons chives and onions into dumpling skin.

"So the ancestors say." Lunha's enemies tend toward a more direct approach. She takes pride in having survived some two hundred assassination attempts, though it doesn't escape her that she might've failed to foil the final one. "These days there are quicker ways."

The cook chuckles like dry clay cracking. "These days you point the young, impressionable son to Pale Cascade."

"Ah, it is but half a chance of ruin. I thought they hosted guests no more, having become grudging on hospitality of late? Since we can't get off-world it was my hope to at least visit every hold before matrimony binds me . . . "

He shrugs, pinches the last dumpling shut, and begins arranging them in the steamer. On Tiansong no one trusts replicants to get cuisine right. "If you know someone who knows someone in Silent Bridge."

"Is that so. Many thanks, uncle."

She catches the next finned, plumaged train bound for her ancestral home.

The public sync, the great shared memory, is an instrument to maintain peace. Even after learning of it and what it does, Lunha continued to believe this, as she does now. It doesn't do much for freedom of thought; it comes with all the downsides of information regulated under the state's clenched fist and the grid usurps perception of the real. But it functions, stabilizes. The Costeya Hegemony has existed in equilibrium for centuries.

It is useful now as she edits herself into the distant branches of Silent Bridge rather than its primary boughs, as her true birth order dictates. The specifics make her hesitate. She settles on female, for convenience more than anything, and picks childless Ninth Aunt as her mother. No sibling, less dissonance to having a sudden sister where once there was none. Those reactions cannot be overridden. Emotions cannot be molded.

When she arrives at the entrance bridge suspended between the maws of pearl-clasping dragons, Ninth Aunt comes to greet her. "My girl," her aunt says uncertainly, "what kept you so long in Razor Garden?"

"Grand nuptials, Mother, and I earned my board helping." A bow, proper. An embrace, stiff. Having a daughter is merely a fact, the gestures Ninth Aunt makes merely obligation.

Her edits have it that she's been away three months; in truth she hasn't been home for as long as—her mind stumbles over the rut of her death. But not counting that it's been five years. Silent Bridge hasn't changed. A central pagoda for common worship. Sapphire arches and garnet gates twining in conversation to mark the city's boundaries. Tiansong cities have always been less crowded than most, and there's never that density of lives in the habitat towers here as on Costeya birthworlds. A wealth of space, a freedom of aesthetics. Barely a whisper of the Hegemony.

Far better off than many Costeya subjects, Lunha knows for a fact; there are border planets that remain in ruins even to this day after their annexation. She cannot understand Xinjia.

When they first met Xinjia wore masks and prosthetic arms; she danced between folded shadows of dragons and herons, only parts of her visible in infrared. Like all thespians of her caliber, Xinjia never appeared in off-world broadcasts. Tiansong makes a fortune out of its insularity—foreigners wishing to enjoy its arts must come to the source and pay dearly, though there are always rogues and imitators.

Lunha in the audience, breathless from applause. A friend who knew a friend brokered her an introduction. Offstage, Xinjia shed the mask but kept the dress, paper breastplate and bladed belts. In the custom of shadow-thespians she wore her face plain, bare, without mods. It made Lunha touch her own, self-conscious of the optic overlays, the duochrome cast to her jawline, replicant-chic.

They talked quickly, amidst the noise of departing spectators; they talked again later, in the quiet of the staff's lounge where the furniture, retrogressive, did not contour to their bodies.

"You talk drama like a layperson," Xinjia remarked once, between sips of liquid gold and jellyfish garnished in diced ivory.

"I don't have a background."

"Officer school doesn't teach fine arts?" The actor drew a finger across Lunha's knuckles. "A soldier with a passion for theater."

"Not before tonight." Lunha caught herself, succeeded in not blushing.

"Soldiers fascinate me," Xinjia said, absently. "The juxtaposition of discipline and danger. Violence and control."

Tiansong marriage lasts five years, at the end of which spouses and family members evaluate one another: how well they fit, how well they belong. A collaborative project.

They wedded on a barge, surrounded by family, blessed by avatars of thundering war-gods with their quadruple arms and spears and battle-wheels. Given that Silent Bridge and Pale Cascade were old rivals, neither Xinjia nor Lunha expected it to last—and it came a surprise to all involved that the marriage was extended past the first five years into the second, then the third.

Divorce came after Lunha made lieutenant-colonel. By then they'd been spouses for nineteen years.

The ivory tiles and the redwood walls of the great house hum with trackers. Lunha sets her array to nullify ones that would gene-match her.

Silent Bridge has always been one of the more—paranoid, she supposes other clans would say—but it's never been like this. A city-wide security lockdown. Anyone not family has been ejected; off-worlders are long gone, scared away by a non-existent epidemic just before the embargo fell.

Xinjia anticipated that sanction. Lunha considers the possibility that she found a way to manipulate the sync. It unsettles.

She keeps up desultory small talk with Ninth Aunt, with cousins who tentatively say they have missed her. It is the thing to say to a relative months unseen. They do it carefully, unsure of the words, of regarding her as family.

To pretend to be a stranger pretending to be of Silent Bridge. Lunha buried away entirely, like the haunting she is, the ghost she should be.

"Is that all you have?" Ninth Aunt says, trying to be a mother. "The clothes on your back and not much else?"

"I've always traveled light." Lunha nods. "You know that, Mother."

"You've never taken care of yourself, more like."

It always surprises Lunha what people imagine to fill up the gaps, patch up the cracks of recall brought by the blunt impact of edit. A defense mechanism, army psychologists liked to tell her, to ward off mental dissolution. There are Hegemonic facilities devoted to research into that, the sync's effects. What it can do. What it can't.

Isren has gifted her with a spy-host; Lunha activates it with a visualization of tadpoles bursting through deep water. She avoids contact. There are disconnected people in Silent Bridge. They would know Ninth Aunt has never had children.

After days of self-imposed house arrest, she steals to the streets.

In the hours of thought and ancestors, the walkways are burnished gold. A low whisper of overhead vehicles like memory, a gleam of pearl from atmospheric stations like moons. Lunha inhales not air but the quiet.

She wanders first aimless, then with a direction as she cross-references the host's eavesdropped data. From the security measures she assumed

25

it would be the great house, the halls in which Silent Bridge primaries make governance and cast laws. Two of them her mothers. They are proud of Lunha, but they always expected her rise through the ranks, her conquests of fifteen worlds in Costeya's name, and if she'd been or done any less it would have been a blot on a lineage of prodigies.

An old shrine, turtle tiles and turtle roof, stone monks enclosing a garden of fern and lavender. The scriptorium is guarded by wasp drones. She inputs a bypass code, stop-motion images of blue heron spearing silver fish. A murmur of acknowledgment and they give way; these are all Hegemonic make, and she has been reinstated as general. They've been reverse-engineered, but not deep enough to keep her out. She can't quite fault the Tiansong techs; less than a thousand in the Hegemony command her level of access.

Between shelves showing paper books in augmens visuals, Lunha waits. She passes the time reading poetry, immersing herself in Huasing's interlocking seven-ten stanzas, Gweilin's interstitial prose-sculpture telling of the sun-archer and her moon-wife. They eel through her awareness, comforting, the balm of familiarity.

Xinjia arrives, eventually. It is where she comes to think when she needs solitude, and from what Lunha can tell solitude is precious to her these days, too rare.

The scriptorium is large, and Lunha did not go sixty years in the army without learning stealth. She finds a space to occupy, a blind spot where Xinjia will not look, and for a time simply observes.

Xinjia looks at peace, striding easily to the mat and the bar. She sheds her slippers, most of her clothes, until she is down to pastel secondskin, lavender shifting to gray as she moves. Hands on the bar she arches backward, stretching until her neck cords, the muscles in her torso pushing out in bas-relief.

Lunha turns off vocal mods and says, in her own voice, "Xinjia."

Her former wife straightens quickly, supple—sinuous. They had elaborate pet names for each other once. Bai Suzhen for Xinjia, after the white snake of legend.

A precipice moment, but Xinjia does not fall. "General Lunha is dead. What are you?"

"A ghost." Lunha reaches into Tiansong's grid. Of course there's a copy of her in the archive of primaries, her knowledge and victories turned to clan wisdom. "But you would be familiar with that."

"Shall I offer you tea?"

"No," Lunha says, though she follows when Xinjia leads her to the low table, the cushions. "How have you been?"

"You'd be familiar with updates on me."

"First of Tiansong."

"It was necessary to obtain that title to do what needs doing." Xinjia calls up the ghost: Lunha's face, serene. Feminine. Xinjia did not much like it when, on rare occasions, Lunha was a man. "This contains much of how you planned, how you dealt with your enemies."

"The data they sent home would be scoured of classified information." A jar of ashes, after a fashion.

"I was more interested in how you thought. Strange, but I don't think I ever knew you so well as posthumously." The secondskin has absorbed sweat, leaves only a trace of clean, saline scent. Xinjia has never worn perfume. Offstage she goes through the world strictly as herself. "There were votes to input your data to a replicant. I overrode it."

"We haven't been spouses for a long time."

"I remarried," Xinjia says, "into Silent Bridge. And so we are family, which gives me some rights over managing your image. Your mothers agreed with me the replicant idea was . . . abhorrent. May I touch you?"

Lunha nods and watches Xinjia's thumb follow the line of her jaw, her nose, her mouth. There Xinjia stops, a weight of consideration, a pressure of shared recall.

"Is it surgery or are you wearing something over your face?"

"The latter," she says against Xinjia's finger and entertains the thought of their first time together, feeding each other slices of persimmon, licking the sweetness off each other's hand. Slick fabrics that warmed to them, braids of sheet slithering against hips and thighs and ankles. For sex Xinjia never liked a still bed. "Why have you undertaken this?"

"A glitch," Xinjia says, in that detached way. Her hand has drifted away to rest—as though incidentally—on Lunha's knee. "A glitch that left some out of sync, myself among them. What was it? Something happening on Yodsana, an explosion at a resort. Just a tidbit of news, insignificant, nothing to do with us. I think I was looking up Yodsana puppet theater, or else I'd never have noticed. To me the resort was operating as usual. To everyone else it'd gone up in flames, fifty tourists dead. I made a note to myself. Except a few days later I couldn't remember why or what it was about. What did I care?"

"That happens." Rarely. Beyond rare.

Xinjia smiles, faint. "I followed some leads, made discoveries, gained contacts. It isn't just me, Lunha. As we speak disconnect is happening on more worlds than you realize, one or two persons at a time. I've only taken it to a larger scale."

"You will take all of Tiansong with you."

"Enough of Tiansong wanted this that they elected me First. Can you imagine how I felt when—" Xinjia blinks, pulls away. A command brings up a floor compartment: a set of cups, a dispenser. "When did they let you . . . ?"

"General. After three successful campaigns." At this point it seems senseless to keep unsaid. "I underwent preparatory conditioning to minimize dissonance, though at the time I didn't realize what it was for."

"Hegemonic personnel must've let it slip. To friends, loved ones."

"Seldom. Easily overwritten." Easily detected. The penalties exorbitant.

"You are all right with this?" Xinjia pours. Chrysanthemum steam, the tea thick with tiny black pearls harvested from Razor Garden orchards. "Sixty years in service, an illustrious career. You can't understand at all why I'm doing this, why others want me to do this?"

"In principle I can guess. In practice—this is not wise."

A cup is slid toward her. "They can take all we are from us. They can rob us of our languages, our cities, our names; they can make us strangers to ourselves and to our ghosts, until there's no one left to tend the altars or follow the hour of thought or sweep the graves."

Lunha sips. She misses touch, not just any human contact but Xinjia's specifically. "The Hegemony has no cause to do that. The amount of rewriting it'd take would be colossal."

"It would cost them less to reduce Tiansong to scorch marks than to process that much. Yes. Should they find a reason though, my soldier, they will do it. Changing us a little at a time. Perhaps one day we'll stop lighting the incenses, the next we'll have Costeya replicants cooking for us. After a month, no one dances anymore the way I do. Instead: Costeya scripts, chrome stages and replicants performers, like on Imral and Salhune. They've this hold on our . . . everything. That I cannot abide." Her former wife, someone else's now, looks up. "I believed that neither would you."

"Xinjia. Bai Suzhen." Lunha does not reach out, still, will not be the one to yield tenderness. They haven't been spouses for so long. "Eighty years ago there was a conflict between Iron Gate and Crimson Falls. It was escalating. It'd have torn Tiansong apart, a field of ruins and carcasses, until the Hegemony intervened. A thorough edit. Now no one remembers that; now Iron Gate and Crimson Falls are at peace. You may not believe it, but that is what soldiers fight for—to preserve equilibrium, to bring stability."

"To enforce the Hegemonic definition of that."

"It's one that works."

"And the massacres of Tiansong empresses when Costeya first took over, what about that? Is that stability; is that peace? Or is it bygones simply because it's been all of three centuries? No. Don't answer that."

"There are planets *now* which suffer much worse. I've been there; I've ordered their ruin and the execution of their citizens." Lunha knows that she has failed, already. That there was never a way to win. Not here.

"You are not yourself," Xinjia says softly.

"I am. I have always been myself."

"Then there is no ground on which we can meet. Perhaps there never has been."

Lunha drinks until there's no more in her cup, tea or pearl. "I will find a way to keep Tiansong safe."

In the end neither of them surrenders. They do not touch; they do not kiss. A parting of strangers' courtesy.

"Isren."

It takes no more than that, on their unique frequency, to summon the operative. A link, with visuals to let her know Isren remains in the habitat. "Yes, General?"

"I could not dissuade First of Tiansong."

"In that case please head for Iron Gate. There'll be a shuttle keyed to one of our ships in orbit."

"No." Lunha gazes out through the round window, makes it widen to take up the whole wall. Silent Bridge at midday is platinum. "Bring me armor. I expect it within seventy-two hours. Are you authorized to officiate a duel?"

Her handler's expression does not change, save for a rapid blink. "That's not what we had in mind, General."

"A duel minimizes collateral damage. Tiansong's representative wins and we leave it under embargo, to limit the influence of disconnect. If Xinjia is assassinated, apprehended or otherwise forcibly stopped there will be others, and not on this world alone. It'll be almost impossible to track the unsynchronized." It is not a certainty, but it is how Xinjia would have learned to plot from Lunha's image. "I win and Tiansong gives up its schemes, surrenders to reintegration. I don't lose, Operative Isren."

"You invoke an archaic statute."

"I invoke it correctly, and this is not the first time I've pushed to resolve by single combat. This is a situation where military destruction is untenable, diplomatic solution impossible."

"If you lose, General, I'll be overriding the result." Isren is silent for a moment. "A duel to the death."

"So it goes."

She sends word to Xinjia to choose a single-combat proxy, briskly outlining the terms. Xinjia accepts them immediately. They are the best that can be had, under the circumstances.

Lunha revokes the edits she made and takes off the facial mesh. She spends some time cleaning, hot water this side of scalding, balm and pigments to smooth away marks left by the mesh. Tiansong commanders of old did that, purify mind and body before going into battle, and Lunha has always followed suit. Not much time for the mind, but few engagements ever gave her the leisure.

Isren's arrival is not covert, and Silent Bridge is prepared. Lunha watches a feed from the operative's eyes as the primaries greet the neutrois, coolly formal. Isren's readouts telling who is disconnected: Lunha's mothers, two other primaries, distant cousins Lunha doesn't know—too young.

They escort Isren, courteous. Lunha does not admit them into her room. Her mothers catch a glimpse of her face—her own, the face she was born and grew up with—and Mother Yinliang's eyes widen, stricken.

Isren unpacks armor, dress uniform, more weapons. "I assumed you'd want this to be ceremonious. I've obtained authorization for your . . . tactical decision."

Perhaps she should've found time to speak to her mothers, Lunha thinks, but it is too late, she moved too fast. Odd, that. In battle there's never been such a thing as *too fast*. "I appreciate it."

"Do you want to talk about it?" Isren tilts their head, just enough to emphasize a pale throat notched by a jeweled implant.

"I don't intend to become familiar with you, Operative."

The neutrois' laugh is ambiguous. "I'm married, quite happily. A career soldier like you, though she's not half as feted. There's an advantage to partnering within the ranks. Fewer secrets to keep. Speaking of that, has the First of Tiansong gone entirely offline, physically removed the neural implants? Can she still interface with the grid?"

"She's kept the implants."

Isren inclines their head. "I've sent you a program. Experimental. It'll reintegrate her into sync. The infiltration method is the best of what we have; all you need is to establish a link with her and it'll latch on."

"Side-effects?" Lunha grips the helm in her hands and decides against it. She'll show her face.

"So far as it's been tested, none. The worst that could happen is that it won't work."

No side-effects. A program that forces neural interface back into the grid, and Isren would have her believe there are no side-effects. Isren wears no immediately visible protection, but they are not without. Lunha calculates her odds of avoiding the nerve toxins and disabling Isren before the operative's nanos activate. Aloud she says only, "I'll take that into account, Operative Isren. My thanks."

At night, Silent Bridge is sapphires. All the colors that sapphires can be, the finest grade and luster.

Under her armor the dress uniform is snug; at her hip the orchid-blade rests with the ease of her own limbs. The winds cut harsh enough to sting and the summit of the great house is sheer, the tiles under them smooth.

Mother Yinliang has no expression anymore; Mother Fangxiu never did. Xinjia merely looks abstract, her gaze apathetic save when it rests on her proxy. A broad woman, sleek and muscled like a fox, veteran champion of Iron Gate pits. An insult, when it comes down to it, though Lunha does not underestimate.

Each pair of eyes records and broadcasts. The uniform, the armor. She is a Hegemonic general. Except for her and Isren there is no hint of Costeya anywhere in Silent Bridge.

Still time to execute that program, General. Isren's voice through the private band.

Lunha strides forward to pay her mothers respect. Bending one knee, head bowed, the submission of a proper child. Neither answers her; neither touches her head. She accepts that and rises to face the pit fighter.

The first trickle of adrenaline. Her reflexes coil and her mind settles into that space of faceted clarity, the interior of her skull arctic and luminous.

She unsheathes her orchid-blade, its mouths baring teeth to the wind, its teeth clicking hunger to the cold.

They begin.

ABOUT THE AUTHOR

Benjanun Sriduangkaew spends her time on amateur photography, makeup, and cities. Her fiction can be found in *GigaNotoSaurus*, *Beneath Ceaseless Skies* and anthologies from Solaris Books and Mythic Delirium.

10^{16} to 1

JAMES PATRICK KELLY

But the best evidence we have that time travel is not possible, and never will be, is that we have not been invaded by hordes of tourists from the future.
—Stephen Hawking, "The Future of the Universe"

I remember now how lonely I was when I met Cross. I never let anyone know about it, because being alone back then didn't make me quite so unhappy. Besides, I was just a kid. I thought it was my own fault.

It looked like I had friends. In 1962, I was on the swim team and got elected Assistant Patrol Leader of the Wolf Patrol in Boy Scout Troop 7. When sides got chosen for kickball at recess, I was usually the fourth or fifth pick. I wasn't the best student in the sixth grade of John Jay Elementary School—that was Betty Garolli. But I was smart and the other kids made me feel bad about it. So I stopped raising my hand when I knew the answer and I watched my vocabulary. I remember I said *albeit* once in class and they teased me for weeks. Packs of girls would come up to me on the playground. "Oh Ray," they'd call and when I turned around they'd scream, "All beat it!" and run away, choking with laughter.

It wasn't that I wanted to be popular or anything. All I really wanted was a friend, one friend, a friend I didn't have to hide anything from. Then came Cross, and that was the end of that.

One of the problems was that we lived so far away from everything. Back then, Westchester County wasn't so suburban. Our house was deep in the woods in tiny Willoughby, New York, at the dead end of Cobb's Hill Road. In the winter, we could see Long Island Sound, a silver needle on the horizon pointing toward the city. But school was a half hour drive away and the nearest kid lived in Ward's Hollow, three miles down the road, and he was a dumb fourth-grader.

So I didn't have any real friends. Instead, I had science fiction. Mom used to complain that I was obsessed. I watched *Superman* reruns every day after school. On Friday nights Dad used to let me stay up for *Twilight Zone,* but that fall CBS had temporarily cancelled it. It came back in January after everything happened, but was never quite the same. On Saturdays, I watched old sci-fi movies on *Adventure Theater.* My favorites were *Forbidden Planet* and *The Day The Earth Stood Still.* I think it was because of the robots. I decided that when I grew up and it was the future, I was going to buy one, so I wouldn't have to be alone anymore.

On Monday mornings I'd get my weekly allowance—a quarter. Usually I'd get off the bus that same afternoon down in Ward's Hollow so I could go to Village Variety. Twenty five cents bought two comics and a pack of red licorice. I especially loved DC's *Green Lantern,* Marvel's *Fantastic Four* and *Incredible Hulk,* but I'd buy almost any superhero. I read all the science fiction books in the library twice, even though Mom kept nagging me to try different things. But what I loved best of all was *Galaxy* magazine. Dad had a subscription and when he was done reading them he would slip them to me. Mom didn't approve. I always used to read them up in the attic or out in the lean-to I'd lashed together in the woods. Afterwards I'd store them under my bunk in the bomb shelter. I knew that after the nuclear war, there would be no TV or radio or anything and I'd need something to keep me busy when I wasn't fighting mutants.

I was too young in 1962 to understand about Mom's drinking. I could see that she got bright and wobbly at night, but she was always up in the morning to make me a hot breakfast before school. And she would have graham crackers and peanut butter waiting when I came home—sometimes cinnamon toast. Dad said I shouldn't ask Mom for rides after five because she got so tired keeping house for us. He sold Andersen windows and was away a lot, so I was pretty much stranded most of the time. But he always made a point of being home on the first Tuesday of the month, so he could take me to the Scout meeting at 7:30.

No, looking back on it, I can't really say that I had an unhappy childhood—until I met Cross.

I remember it was a warm Saturday afternoon in October. The leaves covering the ground were still crisp and their scent spiced the air. I was in the lean-to I'd built that spring, mostly to practice the square and diagonal lashings I needed for Scouts. I was reading *Galaxy.* I even remember the story: "The Ballad of Lost C'Mell" by Cordwainer Smith. The squirrels must have been chittering for some time, but I was too engrossed by Lord Jestocost's problems to notice. Then I heard a faint *crunch,* not ten feet away. I froze, listening. *Crunch, crunch . . .* then silence. It could've been a dog, except that dogs didn't usually slink through the woods. I was hoping it might be a deer—I'd never seen deer in Willoughby before, although I'd heard hunters shooting. I scooted silently across the dirt floor and peered between the dead saplings.

At first I couldn't see anything, which was odd. The woods weren't all that thick and the leaves had long since dropped from the understory brush. I wondered if I had imagined the sounds; it wouldn't have been the first time. Then I heard a twig snap, maybe a foot away. The wall shivered as if something had brushed against it, but there was nothing there. *Nothing.* I might have screamed then, except my throat started to close. I heard whatever it was skulk to the front of the lean-to. I watched in horror as an unseen weight pressed an acorn into the soft earth and then I scrambled back into the farthest corner. That's when I noticed that, when I wasn't looking directly at it, the air where the invisible thing should have been shimmered like a mirage. The lashings that held the frame creaked, as if it were bending over to see what it had caught, getting ready to drag me, squealing, out into the sun and . . .

"Oh, fuck," it said in a high, panicky voice and then it thrashed away into the woods.

In that moment I was transformed—and I suppose that history too was forever changed. I had somehow scared the thing off, twelve-year-old scrawny me! But more important was what it had said. Certainly I was well aware of the existence of the word *fuck* before then, but I had never dared use it myself, nor do I remember hearing it spoken by an adult. A spaz like the Murphy kid might say it under his breath, but he hardly counted. I'd always thought of it as language's atomic bomb; used properly the word should make brains shrivel, eardrums explode. But when the invisible thing said fuck and then *ran away,* it betrayed a vulnerability that made me reckless and more than a little stupid.

"Hey, stop!" I took off in pursuit.

I didn't have any trouble chasing it. The thing was no Davy Crockett; it was noisy and clumsy and slow. I could see a flickery outline as it lumbered along. I closed to within twenty feet and then had to hold back or I would've caught up to it. I had no idea what to do next. We blundered on in slower and slower motion until finally I just stopped.

"W-Wait," I called. "W-What do you want?" I put my hands on my waist and bent over like I was trying to catch my breath, although I didn't need to.

The thing stopped too but didn't reply. Instead it sucked air in wheezy, ragged *hooofs*. It was harder to see, now that it was standing still, but I think it must have turned toward me.

"Are you okay?" I said.

"You are a child." It spoke with an odd, chirping kind of accent. Child was *Ch-eye-eld*.

"I'm in the sixth grade." I straightened, spread my hands in front of me to show that I wasn't a threat. "What's your name?" It didn't answer. I took a step toward it and waited. Still nothing, but at least it didn't bolt. "I'm Ray Beaumont," I said finally. "I live over there." I pointed. "How come I can't see you?"

"What is the date?" It said *da-ate-eh*.

For a moment I thought it meant data. Data? I puzzled over an answer. I didn't want it thinking I was just a stupid little kid. "I don't know," I said cautiously. "October twentieth?"

The thing considered this, then asked a question that took my breath away. "And what is the year?"

"Oh jeez," I said. At that point I wouldn't have been surprised if Rod Serling himself had popped out from behind a tree and started addressing the unseen TV audience. Which might have included me, except this was really *happening*. "Do you know what you just . . . what it means when . . . ?"

"What, what?" Its voice rose in alarm.

"You're invisible and you don't know what year it is? Everyone knows what year it is. Are you . . . you're not from here."

"Yes, yes, I am. 1962, of course. This is 1962." It paused. "And I am not invisible." It squeezed about eight syllables into invisible. I heard a sound like paper ripping. "This is only camel." Or at least, that's what I thought it said.

"Camel?"

"No, camo." The air in front of me crinkled and slid away from a dark face. "You have not heard of camouflage?"

"Oh sure, camo."

I suppose the thing meant to reassure me by showing itself, but the effect was just the opposite. Yes, it had two eyes, a nose, and a mouth. It stripped off the camouflage to reveal a neatly-pressed gray three-piece business suit, a white shirt and a red and blue striped tie. At night, on a crowded street in Manhattan, I might've passed it right by—Dad had taught me not to stare at the kooks in the city. But in the afternoon light, I could see all the things wrong with its disguise. The hair, for example. Not exactly a crewcut, it was more of a stubble, like Mr. Rudowski's chin when he was growing his beard. The thing was way too thin, its skin was shiny, its fingers too long and its face—it looked like one of those Barbie dolls.

"Are you a boy or a girl?" I said.

It started. "There is something wrong?"

I cocked my head to one side. "I think maybe it's your eyes. They're too big or something. Are you wearing makeup?"

"I am naturally male." It—he bristled as he stepped out of the camouflage suit. "Eyes do not have gender."

"If you say so." I could see he was going to need help getting around, only he didn't seem to know it. I was hoping he'd reveal himself, brief me on the mission. I even had an idea how we could contact President Kennedy or whoever he needed to meet with. Mr. Newell, the Scoutmaster, used to be a colonel in the Army—he would know some general who could call the Pentagon. "What's your name?" I said.

He draped the suit over his arm. "Cross."

I waited for the rest of it as he folded the suit in half. "Just Cross?" I said.

"My given name is Chitmansing." He warbled it like he was calling birds.

"That's okay," I said. "Let's just make it Mr. Cross."

"As you wish, Mr. Beaumont." He folded the suit again, again and *again*.

"Hey!"

He continued to fold it.

"How do you do that? Can I see?"

He handed it over. The camo suit was more impossible than it had been when it was invisible. He had reduced it to a six-inch square card, as thin and flexible as the queen of spades. I folded it in half myself. The two sides seemed to meld together; it would've fit into my wallet perfectly. I wondered if Cross knew how close I was to running off with his amazing gizmo. He'd never catch me. I could see flashes of my brilliant career as the invisible superhero. *Tales to Confound* presents: the origin of Camo Kid! I turned the card over and over, trying to figure out how to unfold it again. There was no seam, no latch. How could I use it if I couldn't open it? "Neat," I said. Reluctantly, I gave the card back to him.

Besides, real superheroes didn't steal their powers.

I watched Cross slip the card into his vest pocket. I wasn't scared of him. What scared me was that at any minute he might walk out of my life. I had to find a way to tell him I was on his side, whatever that was.

"So you live around here, Mr. Cross?"

"I am from the island of Mauritius."

"Where's that?"

"It is in the Indian Ocean, Mr. Beaumont, near Madagascar."

I knew where Madagascar was from playing *Risk,* so I told him that but then I couldn't think of what else to say. Finally, I had to blurt out something—anything—to fill the silence. "It's nice here. Real quiet, you know. Private."

"Yes, I had not expected to meet anyone." He, too, seemed at a loss. "I have business in New York City on the twenty-sixth of October."

"New York, that's a ways away."

"Is it? How far would you say?"

"Fifty miles. Sixty, maybe. You have a car?"

"No, I do not drive, Mr. Beaumont. I am to take the train."

The nearest train station was New Canaan, Connecticut. I could've hiked it in maybe half a day. It would be dark in a couple of hours. "If your business isn't until the twenty-sixth, you'll need a place to stay."

"The plan is to take rooms at a hotel in Manhattan."

"That costs money."

He opened a wallet and showed me a wad of crisp new bills. For a minute I thought they must be counterfeit; I hadn't realized that Ben Franklin's picture was on money. Cross was giving me the goofiest grin. I just knew they'd eat him alive in New York and spit out the bones.

"Are you sure you want to stay in a hotel?" I said.

He frowned. "Why would I not?"

"Look, you need a friend, Mr. Cross. Things are different here than . . . than on your island. Sometimes people do, you know, bad stuff. Especially in the city."

He nodded and put his wallet away. "I am aware of the dangers, Mr. Beaumont. I have trained not to draw attention to myself. I have the proper equipment." He tapped the pocket where the camo was.

I didn't point out to him that all his training and equipment hadn't kept him from being caught out by a twelve-year-old. "Sure, okay. It's just . . . Look, I have a place for you to stay, if you want. No one will know."

"Your parents, Mr. Beaumont . . ."

"My dad's in Massachusetts until next Friday. He travels; he's in the window business. And my mom won't know."

"How can she not know that you have invited a stranger into your house?"

"Not the house," I said. "My dad built us a bomb shelter. You'll be safe there, Mr. Cross. It's the safest place I know."

I remember how Cross seemed to lose interest in me, his mission and the entire twentieth century the moment he entered the shelter. He sat around all of Sunday, dodging my attempts to draw him out. He seemed distracted, like he was listening to a conversation I couldn't hear. When he wouldn't talk, we played games. At first it was cards: Gin and Crazy Eights, mostly. In the afternoon, I went back to the house and brought over checkers and *Monopoly*. Despite the fact that he did not seem to be paying much attention, he beat me like a drum. Not one game was even close. But that wasn't what bothered me. I believed that this man had come from the future, and here I was building hotels on Baltic Avenue!

Monday was a school day. I thought Cross would object to my plan of locking him in and taking both my key and Mom's key with me, but he never said a word. I told him that it was the only way I could be sure that Mom didn't catch him by surprise. Actually, I doubted she'd come all the way out to the shelter. She'd stayed away after Dad gave her that first tour; she had about as much use for nuclear war as she had for science fiction. Still, I had no idea what she did during the day while I was gone. I couldn't take chances. Besides, it was a good way to make sure that Cross didn't skin out on me.

Dad had built the shelter instead of taking a vacation in 1960, the year Kennedy beat Nixon. It was buried about a hundred and fifty feet from the house. Nothing special—just a little cellar without anything built on top of it. The entrance was a steel bulkhead that led down five steps to another steel door. The inside was cramped; there were a couple of cots, a sink and a toilet. Almost half of the space was filled with supplies and equipment. There were no windows and it always smelled a little musty, but I loved going down there to pretend the bombs were falling.

When I opened the shelter door after school on that Monday, Cross lay just as I had left him the night before, sprawled across the big cot, staring at nothing. I remember being a little worried; I thought he might be sick. I stood beside him and still he didn't acknowledge my presence.

"Are you all right, Mr. Cross?" I said. "I bought *Risk*." I set it next to him on the bed and nudged him with the corner of the box to wake him up. "Did you eat?"

He sat up, took the cover off the game and started reading the rules. "President Kennedy will address the nation," he said, "this evening at seven o'clock."

For a moment, I thought he had made a slip. "How do you know that?"

"The announcement came last night." I realized that his pronunciation had improved a lot; *announcement* had only three syllables. "I have been studying the radio."

I walked over to the radio on the shelf next to the sink. Dad said we were supposed to leave it unplugged—something about the bombs making a power surge. It was a brand new solid-state, multi-band Heathkit that I'd helped him build. When I pressed the on button, women immediately started singing about shopping: *Where the values go up, up, up! And the prices go down, down, down!* I turned it off again.

"Do me a favor, okay?" I said. "Next time when you're done would you please unplug this? I could get in trouble if you don't." I stooped to yank the plug.

When I stood up, he was holding a sheet of paper. "I will need some things tomorrow, Mr. Beaumont. I would be grateful if you could assist me."

I glanced at the list without comprehension. He must have typed it, only there was no typewriter in the shelter.

To buy:
- One General Electric transistor radio with earplug
- One General Electric replacement earplug
- Two Eveready Heavy Duty nine volt batteries
- One *New York Times,* Tuesday, October 23
- Rand McNally map of New York City and vicinity

To receive in change:
- Five dollars in coins
- Twenty nickels
- Ten dimes
- Twelve quarters

When I looked up, I could feel the change in him. His gaze was electric; it seemed to crackle down my nerves. I could tell that what I did next would matter very much. "I don't get it," I said.

"There are inaccuracies?"

I tried to stall. "Look, you'll pay almost double if we buy a transistor radio at Ward's Hollow. I'll have to buy it at Village Variety. Wait a couple of days—we can get one much cheaper down in Stamford."

"My need is immediate." He extended his hand and tucked something into the pocket of my shirt. "I am assured this will cover the expense."

I was afraid to look, even though I knew what it was. He'd given me a hundred dollar bill. I tried to thrust it back at him but he stepped away and it spun to the floor between us. "I can't spend that."

"You must read your own money, Mr. Beaumont." He picked the bill up and brought it into the light of the bare bulb on the ceiling. "This note is legal tender for all debts public and private."

"No, no, you don't understand. A kid like me doesn't walk into Village Variety with a hundred bucks. Mr. Rudowski will call my mom!"

"If it is inconvenient for you, I will secure the items myself." He offered me the money again.

If I didn't agree, he'd leave and probably never come back. I was getting mad at him. Everything would be so much easier if only he'd admit what we both knew about who he was. Then I could do whatever he wanted with a clear conscience. Instead he was keeping all the wrong secrets and acting really weird. It made me feet dirty, like I was helping a pervert. "What's going on," I said.

"I do not know how to respond, Mr. Beaumont. You have the list. Read it now and tell me please with which item you have a problem."

I snatched the hundred dollars from him and jammed it into my pants pocket. "Why don't you trust me?"

He stiffened as if I had hit him.

"I let you stay here. I didn't tell anyone. You have to give me *something,* Mr. Cross."

"Well then . . . " He looked uncomfortable. "I would ask you to keep the change."

"Oh jeez, thanks." I snorted in disgust. "Okay, okay, I'll buy this stuff right after school tomorrow."

With that, he seemed to lose interest again. When we opened the *Risk* board, he showed me where his island was, except it wasn't there because it was too small. We played three games and he crushed me every time. I remember at the end of the last game, watching in disbelief as he finished building a wall of invading armies along the shores of North Africa. South America, my last continent, was doomed. "Looks like you win again," I said. I traded in the last of my cards for new armies and launched a final, useless counter-attack. When I was done, he studied the board for a moment.

"I think *Risk* is not a proper simulation, Mr. Beaumont. We should both lose for fighting such a war."

"That's crazy," I said. "Both sides can't lose."

"Yet they can," he said. "It sometimes happens that the victors envy the dead."

That night was the first time I can remember being bothered by Mom talking back to the TV. I used to talk to the TV too. When Buffalo Bob asked what time it was, I would screech *It's Howdy Doody Time* just like every other kid in America.

"My fellow citizens," said President Kennedy, "let no one doubt that this is a difficult and dangerous effort on which we have set out." I thought the president looked tired, like Mr. Newell on the third day of a campout. "No one can foresee precisely what course it will take or what costs or casualties will be incurred."

"Oh my god," Mom screamed at him. "You're going to kill us all!"

Despite the fact that it was close to her bedtime and she was shouting at the President of the United States, Mom looked great. She was wearing a shiny black dress and a string of pearls. She always got dressed up at night, whether Dad was home or not. I suppose most kids don't notice how their mothers look, but everyone always said how beautiful Mom was. And since Dad thought so too, I went along with it—as long as she didn't open her mouth. The problem was that a lot of the time, Mom didn't make any sense. When she embarrassed me, it didn't matter how pretty she was. I just wanted to crawl behind the couch.

"*Mom.*"

As she leaned toward the television, the martini in her glass came close to slopping over the edge.

President Kennedy stayed calm. "The path we have chosen for the present is full of hazards, as all paths are—but it is the one most consistent with our character and courage as a nation and our commitments around the world. The cost of freedom is always high—but Americans have always paid it. And one path we shall never choose, and that is the path of surrender or submission."

"Shut up! You foolish man, *stop this.*" She shot out of her chair and then some of her drink did spill. "Oh, damn!"

"Take it easy, Mom."

"Don't you understand?" She put the glass down and tore a Kleenex from the box on the end table. "He wants to start World War III!" She dabbed at the front of her dress and the phone rang.

I said, "Mom, nobody wants World War III."

She ignored me, brushed by and picked up the phone on the third ring.

"Oh thank God," she said. I could tell from the sound of her voice that it was Dad. "You heard him then?" She bit her lip as she listened to him. "Yes, but . . ."

Watching her face made me sorry I was in the sixth grade. Better to be a stupid little kid again, who thought grownups knew everything. I wondered whether Cross had heard the speech.

"No, I can't, Dave. No." She covered the phone with her hand. "Raymie, turn off that TV!"

I hated it when she called me Raymie, so I only turned the sound down.

"You have to come home now, Dave. No, you listen to *me*. Can't you see, the man's obsessed? Just because he has a grudge against Castro doesn't mean he's allowed to . . ."

With the sound off, Chet Huntley looked as if he were speaking at his own funeral.

"I am *not* going in there without you."

I think Dad must have been shouting because Mom held the receiver away from her ear.

She waited for him to calm down and said, "And neither is Raymie. He'll stay with me."

"Let me talk to him," I said. I bounced off the couch. The look she gave me stopped me dead.

"What for?" she said to Dad. "No, we are going to finish this conversation, David, do you hear me?"

She listened for a moment. "Okay, all right, but don't you dare hang up." She waved me over and slapped the phone into my hand as if I had put the missiles in Cuba. She stalked to the kitchen.

I needed a grownup so bad that I almost cried when I heard Dad's voice. "Ray," he said, "your mother is pretty upset."

"Yes," I said.

"I want to come home—I *will* come home—but I can't just yet. If I just up and leave and this blows over, I'll get fired."

"But, Dad . . ."

"You're in charge until I get there. Understand, son? If the time comes, everything is up to you."

"Yes, sir," I whispered. I'd heard what he didn't say—it wasn't up to *her*.

"I want you to go out to the shelter tonight. Wait until she goes to sleep. Top off the water drums. Get all the gas out of the garage and store it next to the generator. But here's the most important thing. You know the sacks of rice? Drag them off to one side, the pallet too. There's a hatch underneath, the key to the airlock door unlocks it. You've got two new guns and plenty of ammunition. The revolver is a .357 Magnum. You be careful with that, Ray, it can blow a hole in a car but it's hard to aim. The double-barreled shotgun is easy to aim but you have to be close to do any harm. And I want you to bring down the Gamemaster from my closet and the .38 from my dresser drawer." He had been talking as if there would be no tomorrow; he paused then to catch his breath. "Now, this is all just in case, okay? I just want you to know."

I had never been so scared in my life.

"Ray?"

I should have told him about Cross then, but Mom weaved into the room. "Got it, Dad," I said. "Here she is."

Mom smiled at me. It was a lopsided smile that was trying to be brave but wasn't doing a very good job of it. She had a new glass and it was full. She held out her hand for the phone and I gave it to her.

I remember waiting until almost ten o'clock that night, reading under the covers with a flashlight. The Fantastic Four invaded Latveria to defeat Doctor Doom; Superman tricked Mr. Mxyzptlk into saying his name backwards once again. When I opened the door to my parents' bedroom, I could hear Mom snoring. It spooked me; I hadn't realized that women did that. I thought about sneaking in to get the guns, but decided to take care of them tomorrow.

I stole out to the shelter, turned my key in the lock and pulled on the bulkhead door. It didn't move. That didn't make any sense, so I gave it a hard yank. The steel door rattled terribly but did not swing away. The air had turned frosty and the sound carried in the cold. I held my breath, listening to my blood pound. The house stayed dark, the shelter quiet as stones. After a few moments, I tried one last time before I admitted to myself what had happened.

Cross had bolted the door shut from the inside.

I went back to my room, but couldn't sleep. I kept going to the window to watch the sky over New York, waiting for a flash of killing light. I was all but convinced that the city would burn that very night in thermo-nuclear fire and that mom and I would die horrible deaths soon after, pounding on the unyielding steel doors of our shelter. Dad had left me in charge and I had let him down.

I didn't understand why Cross had locked us out. If he knew that a nuclear war was about to start, he might want our shelter all to himself. But that made him a monster and I still didn't see him as a monster. I tried to tell myself that he'd been asleep and couldn't hear me at the door—but that couldn't be right. What if he'd come to prevent the war? He'd said he had business in the city on Thursday; he could be doing something really, really futuristic in there that he couldn't let me see. Or else he was having problems. Maybe our twentieth century germs had got to him, like they killed H. G. Wells's Martians.

I must have teased a hundred different ideas apart that night, in between uneasy trips to the window and glimpses at the clock. The last time I remember seeing was 4:16. I tried to stay up to face the end, but I couldn't.

I wasn't dead when I woke up the next morning, so I had to go to school. Mom had Cream of Wheat all ready when I dragged myself to the table. Although she was all bright and bubbly, I could feel her giving me the mother's eye when I wasn't looking. She always knew when something was wrong. I tried not to show her anything. There was no time to sneak out to the shelter; I barely had time to finish eating before she bundled me off to the bus.

Right after the morning bell, Miss Toohey told us to open *The Story of New York State* to Chapter Seven, *Resources and Products* and read to ourselves. Then she left the room. We looked at each other in amazement. I heard Bobby Coniff whisper something. It was probably dirty; a few kids snickered. Chapter Seven started with a map of product symbols. Two teeny little cows grazed near Binghamton. Rochester was cog and a pair of glasses. Elmira was an adding machine, Oswego an apple. There was a lightning bolt over Niagara Falls. Dad had promised to take us there someday. I had the sick feeling that we'd never get the chance. Miss Toohey looked pale when she came back, but that didn't stop her from giving us a spelling test. I got a ninety-five. The word I spelled wrong was *enigma.* The hot lunch was American Chop Suey, a roll, a salad and a bowl of butterscotch pudding. In the afternoon we did decimals.

Nobody said anything about the end of the world.

I decided to get off the bus in Ward's Hollow, buy the stuff Cross wanted and pretend I didn't know he had locked the shelter door last night. If he said something about it, I'd act surprised. If he didn't . . . I didn't know what I'd do then.

Village Variety was next to Warren's Esso and across the street from the Post Office. It had once been two different stores located in the same building, but then Mr. Rudowski had bought the building and knocked down the dividing wall. On the fun side were pens and pencil and paper and greeting cards and magazines and comics and paperbacks and candy. The other side was all boring hardware and small appliances.

Mr. Rudowski was on the phone when I came in, but then he was always on the phone when he worked. He could sell you a hammer or a pack of baseball cards, tell you a joke, ask about your family, complain about the weather and still keep the guy on the other end of the line happy. This time though, when he saw me come in, he turned away, wrapping the phone cord across his shoulder.

I went through the store quickly and found everything Cross had wanted. I had to blow dust off the transistor radio box but the batteries looked fresh. There was only one *New York Times* left; the headlines were so big they were scary.

US IMPOSES ARMS BLOCKADE ON CUBA ON FINDING OF OFFENSIVE MISSILE SITES; KENNEDY READY FOR SOVIET SHOWDOWN

Ships Must Stop   President Grave   Prepared To Risk War.

I set my purchases on the counter in front of Mr. Rudowski. He cocked his head to one side, trapping the telephone receiver against his shoulder, and rang me up. The paper was on the bottom of the pile.

"Since when do you read the *Times*, Ray?" Mr. Rudowski punched it into the cash register and hit total. "I just got the new *Fantastic Four*." The cash drawer popped open.

"Maybe tomorrow," I said.

"All right then. It comes to twelve dollars and forty-seven cents."

I gave him the hundred dollar bill.

"What is this, Ray?" He stared at it and then at me.

I had my story all ready. "It was a birthday gift from my grandma in Detroit. She said I could spend it on whatever I wanted so I decided to treat myself but I'm going to put the rest in the bank."

"You're buying a radio? From me?"

"Well, you know. I thought maybe I should have one with me with all this stuff going on."

He didn't say anything for a moment. He just pulled a paper bag from under the counter and put my things into it. His shoulders were hunched; I thought maybe he felt guilty about overcharging for the radio. "You should be listening to music, Ray," he said quietly. "You like Elvis? All kids like Elvis. Or maybe that colored, the one who does the Twist?"

"They're all right, I guess."

"You're too young to be worrying about the news. You hear me? Those politicians . . ." He shook his head. "It's going to be okay, Ray. You heard it from me."

"Sure, Mr. Rudowski. I was wondering, could I get five dollars in change?"

I could feel him watching me as I stuffed it all into my book bag. I was certain he'd call my mom, but he never did. Home was three miles up Cobb's Hill. I did it in forty minutes, a record.

• • •

I remember I started running when I saw the flashing lights. The police car had left skid marks in the gravel on our driveway.

"Where were you?" Mom burst out of the house as I came across the lawn. "Oh, my God, Raymie, I was worried sick." She caught me up in her arms.

"I got off the bus in Ward's Hollow." She was about to smother me; I squirmed free. "What happened?"

"This the boy, ma'am?" The state trooper had taken his time catching up to her. He had almost the same hat as Scoutmaster Newell.

"Yes, yes! Oh, thank God, officer!"

The trooper patted me on the head like I was a lost dog. "You had your mom worried, Ray."

"Raymie, you should've told me."

"Somebody tell me what happened!" I said.

A second trooper came from behind the house. We watched him approach. "No sign of any intruder." He looked bored: I wanted to scream.

"Intruder?" I said.

"He broke into the shelter," said Mom. "He knew my name."

"There was no sign of forcible entry," said the second trooper. I saw him exchange a glance with his partner. "Nothing disturbed that I could see."

"He didn't have time," Mom said. "When I found him in the shelter, I ran back to the house and got your father's gun from the bedroom."

The thought of Mom with the .38 scared me. I had my Shooting merit badge, but she didn't know a hammer from a trigger. "You didn't shoot him?"

"No." She shook her head. "He had plenty of time to leave but he was still there when I came back. That's when he said my name."

I had never been so mad at her before. "You never go out to the shelter."

She had that puzzled look she always gets at night. "I couldn't find my key. I had to use the one your father leaves over the breezeway door."

"What did he say again, ma'am? The intruder."

"He said, 'Mrs. Beaumont, I present no danger to you.' And I said, 'Who are you?' And then he came toward me and I thought he said 'Margaret,' and I started firing."

"You did shoot him!"

Both troopers must have heard the panic in my voice. The first one said, "You know something about this man, Ray?"

"No, I-I was at school all day and then I stopped at Rudowski's . . ." I could feel my eyes burning. I was so embarrassed; I knew I was about to cry in front of them.

Mom acted annoyed that the troopers had stopped paying attention to her. "I shot *at* him. Three, four times, I don't know. I must have missed, because he just stood there staring at me. It seemed like forever. Then he walked past me and up the stairs like nothing had happened."

"And he didn't say anything?"

"Not a word."

"Well, it beats me," said the second trooper. "The gun's been fired four times but there are no bullet holes in the shelter and no bloodstains."

"You mind if I ask you a personal question, Mrs. Beaumont?" the first trooper said.

She colored. "I suppose not."

"Have you been drinking, ma'am?"

"Oh that!" She seemed relieved. "No. Well, I mean, after I called you, I did pour myself a little something. Just to steady my nerves. I was worried because my son was so late and . . . Raymie, what's the matter?"

I felt so small. The tears were pouring down my face.

After the troopers left, I remember Mom baking brownies while I watched *Superman*. I wanted to go out and hunt for Cross, but it was already sunset and there was no excuse I could come up with for wandering around in the dark. Besides, what was the point? He was gone, driven off by my mother. I'd had a chance to help a man from the future change history, maybe prevent World War III, and I had blown it. My life was ashes.

I wasn't hungry that night, for brownies or spaghetti or anything, but Mom made that clucking noise when I pushed supper around the plate, so I ate a few bites just to shut her up. I was surprised at how easy it was to hate her, how good it felt. Of course, she was oblivious, but in the morning she would notice if I wasn't careful. After dinner she watched the news and I went upstairs to read. I wrapped a pillow around my head when she yelled at David Brinkley. I turned out the lights at 8:30, but I couldn't get to sleep. She went to her room a little after that.

"Mr. Beaumont?"

I must have dozed off, but when I heard his voice I snapped awake immediately.

"Is that you, Mr. Cross?" I peered into the darkness. "I bought the stuff you wanted." The room filled with an awful stink, like when Mom drove with the parking brake on.

"Mr. Beaumont," he said, "I am damaged."

I slipped out of bed, picked my way across the dark room, locked the door and turned on the light.

"Oh jeez!"

He slumped against my desk like a nightmare. I remember thinking then that Cross wasn't human, that maybe he wasn't even alive. His proportions were wrong: an ear, a shoulder and both feet sagged like they had melted. Little wisps of steam or something curled off him; they were what smelled. His skin had gone all shiny and hard; so had his business suit. I'd wondered why he never took the suit coat off and now I knew. His clothes were part of him. The middle fingers of his right hand beat spasmodically against his palm.

"Mr. Beaumont," he said. "I calculate your chances at 10^{16} to 1."

"Chances of what?" I said. "What happened to you?"

"You must listen most attentively, Mr. Beaumont. My decline is very bad for history. It is for you now to alter the time line probabilities."

"I don't understand."

"Your government greatly overestimates the nuclear capability of the Soviet Union. If you originate a first strike, the United States will achieve overwhelming victory."

"Does the President know this? We have to tell him!"

"John Kennedy will not welcome such information. If he starts this war, he will be responsible for the deaths of tens of millions, both Russians and Americans. But he does not grasp the future of the arms race. The war must happen now, because those who come after will build and build until they control arsenals which can destroy the world many times over. People are not capable of thinking for very long of such fearsome weapons. They tire of the idea of extinction and then become numb to it. The buildup slows but does not stop and they congratulate themselves on having survived it. But there are still too many weapons and they never go away. The Third War comes as a surprise. The First War was called the one to end all wars. The Third War is the only such war possible, Mr. Beaumont, because it ends everything. History stops in 2019. Do you understand? A year later, there is no life. All dead, the world a hot, barren rock."

"But you . . . ?"

"I am nothing, a construct. Mr. Beaumont, please, the chances are 10^{16} to 1," he said. "Do you know how improbable that is?" His laugh sounded like a hiccup. "But for the sake of those few precious time lines, we must continue. There is a man, a politician in New York. If he dies on Thursday night, it will create the incident that forces Kennedy's hand."

"Dies?" For days, I had been desperate for him to talk. Now all I wanted was to run away. "You're going to kill somebody?"

"The world will survive a Third War that starts on Friday, October 22, 1962."

"What about me? My parents? Do we survive?"

"I cannot access that time line. I have no certain answer for you. Please, Mr. Beaumont, this politician will die of a heart attack in less than three years. He has made no great contribution to history, yet his assassination can save the world."

"What do you want from me?" But I had already guessed.

"He will speak most eloquently at the United Nations on Friday evening. Afterward he will have dinner with his friend, Ruth Fields. Around ten o'clock he will return to his residence at the Waldorf Towers. Not the Waldorf Astoria Hotel, but the Towers. He will take the elevator to Suite 42A. He is the American ambassador to the United Nations. His name is Adlai Stevenson."

"Stop it! Don't say anything else."

When he sighed, his breath was a cloud of acrid steam. "I have based my calculation of the time line probabilities on two data points, Mr. Beaumont, which I discovered in your bomb shelter. The first is the .357 Magnum revolver, located under a pallet of rice bags. I trust you know of this weapon?"

"Yes," I whispered.

"The second is the collection of magazines, located under your cot. It would seem that you take a interest in what is to come, Mr. Beaumont, and that may lend you the terrible courage you will need to divert this time line from disaster. You should know that there is not just one future. There are an infinite number of futures in which all possibilities are expressed, an infinite number of Raymond Beaumonts."

"Mr. Cross, I can't . . ."

"Perhaps not," he said, "but I believe that another one of you can."

"You don't understand . . ." I watched in horror as a boil swelled on the side of his face and popped, expelling an evil jet of yellow steam. "What?"

"Oh *fuck*." That was the last thing he said.

He slid to the floor—or maybe he was just a body at that point. More boils formed and burst. I opened all the windows in my room and got the fan down out of the closet and still I can't believe that the stink didn't wake Mom up. Over the course of the next few hours, he sort of vaporized.

When it was over, there was a sticky, dark spot on the floor the size of my pillow. I moved the throw rug from one side of the room to the other to cover it up. I had nothing to prove that Cross existed but a transistor radio, a couple of batteries, an earplug and eighty-seven dollars and fifty-three cents in change.

I might have done things differently if I hadn't had a day to think. I can't remember going to school on Wednesday, who I talked to, what I ate. I was feverishly trying to figure out what to do and how to do it. I had no place to go for answers, not Miss Toohey, not my parents, not the Bible or the *Boy Scout Handbook,* certainly not *Galaxy* magazine. Whatever I did had to come out of me. I watched the news with Mom that night. President Kennedy had brought our military to the highest possible state of alert. There were reports that some Russian ships had turned away from Cuba; others continued on course. Dad called and said his trip was being cut short and that he would be home the next day.

But that was too late.

I hid behind the stone wall when the school bus came on Thursday morning. Mrs. Johnson honked a couple of times, and then drove on. I set out for New Canaan, carrying my bookbag. In it were the radio, the batteries, the coins, the map of New York and the .357. I had the rest of Cross's money in my wallet.

It took more than five hours to hike to the train station. I expected to be scared, but the whole time I felt light as air. I kept thinking of what Cross had said about the future, that I was just one of millions and millions of Raymond Beaumonts. Most of them were in school, diagramming sentences and watching Miss Toohey bite her nails. I was the special one, walking into history. I was super. I caught the 2:38 train, changed in Stamford, and arrived at Grand Central just after four. I had six hours. I bought myself a hot pretzel and a Coke and tried to decide where I should go. I couldn't just sit around the hotel lobby for all that time; I thought that would draw too much attention. I decided to go to the top of the Empire State Building. I took my time walking down Park Avenue and tried not to see all the ghosts I was about to make. In the lobby of the Empire State Building, I used Cross's change to call home.

"Hello?" I hadn't expected Dad to answer. I would've hung up except that I knew I might never speak to him again.

"Dad, this is Ray. I'm safe, don't worry."

"Ray, where are you?"

"I can't talk. I'm safe but I won't be home tonight. Don't worry."

"Ray!" He was frantic. "What's going on?"

"I'm sorry."

"Ray!"

I hung up; I had to. "I love you," I said to the dial tone.

I could imagine the expression on Dad's face, how he would tell Mom what I'd said. Eventually they would argue about it. He would shout; she would cry. As I rode the elevator up, I got mad at them. He shouldn't have picked up the phone. They should've protected me from Cross and the future he came from. I was in the sixth grade, I shouldn't have to have feelings like this. The observation platform was almost deserted. I walked completely around it, staring at the city stretching away from me in every direction. It was dusk; the buildings were shadows in the failing light. I didn't feel like Ray Beaumont anymore; he was my secret identity. Now I was the superhero Bomb Boy; I had the power of bringing nuclear war. Wherever I cast my terrible gaze, cars melted and people burst into flame.

And I loved it.

It was dark when I came down from the Empire State Building. I had a sausage pizza and a Coke on 47th Street. While I ate, I stuck the plug into my ear and listened to the radio. I searched for the news. One announcer said the debate was still going on in the Security Council. Our ambassador was questioning Ambassador Zorin. I stayed with that station for a while, hoping to hear his voice. I knew what he looked like, of course. I knew Adlai Stevenson had run for President a couple of times when I was just a baby. But I couldn't remember what he sounded like. He might talk to me, ask me what I was doing in his hotel; I wanted to be ready for that.

I arrived at the Waldorf Towers around nine o'clock. I picked a plush velvet chair that had a direct view of the elevator bank and sat there for about ten minutes. Nobody seemed to care but it was hard to sit still. Finally I got up and went to the men's room. I took my bookbag into a stall, closed the door and got the .357 out. I aimed it at the toilet. The gun was heavy and I could tell it would have a big kick. I probably ought to hold it with both hands. I put it back into my bookbag and flushed.

When I came out of the bathroom, I had stopped believing that I was going to shoot anyone, that I could. But I had to find out for Cross's sake. If I was really meant to save the world, then I had to be in the right place at the right time. I went back to my chair, checked my watch. It was nine-twenty.

I started thinking of the one who would pull the trigger, the unlikely Ray. What would make the difference? Had he read some story in *Galaxy* that I had skipped? Was it a problem with Mom? Or Dad? Maybe he had spelled enigma right; maybe Cross had lived another thirty seconds in his time line. Or maybe he was just the best that I could possibly be.

I was so tired of it all. I must have walked thirty miles since morning and I hadn't slept well in days. The lobby was warm. People laughed and murmured. Elevator doors dinged softly. I tried to stay up to face history, but I couldn't. I was Raymond Beaumont, but I was just a twelve-year-old kid.

I remember the doorman waking me up at eleven o'clock. Dad drove all the way into the city that night to get me. When we got home, Mom was already in the shelter.

Only the Third War didn't start that night. Or the next.

I lost television privileges for a month.

For most people my age, the most traumatic memory of growing up came on November 22, 1963. But the date I remember is July 14, 1965, when Adlai Stevenson dropped dead of a heart attack in London.

I've tried to do what I can, to make up for what I didn't do that night. I've worked for the cause wherever I could find it. I belong to CND and SANE and the Friends of the Earth and was active in the nuclear freeze movement. I think the Green Party (www.greens.org) is the only political organization worth your vote. I don't know if any of it will change Cross's awful probabilities; maybe we'll survive in a few more time lines.

When I was a kid, I didn't mind being lonely. Now it's hard, knowing what I know. Oh, I have lots of friends, all of them wonderful people, but people who know me say that there's a part of myself that I always keep hidden. They're right. I don't think I'll ever be able to tell anyone about what happened with Cross, what I didn't do that night. It wouldn't be fair to them.

Besides, whatever happens, chances are very good that it's my fault.

First published in *Asimov's Science Fiction,* June 1999.

ABOUT THE AUTHOR

James Patrick Kelly made his first sale in 1975, and since has gone on to become one of the most respected and popular writers to enter the field in the last twenty years. Although Kelly has had some success with novels, he has perhaps had more impact to date as a writer of short fiction, and is often ranked among the best short story writers in the business. His story "Think Like a Dinosaur" won him a Hugo Award in 1996, as did his story "10^{16} to 1," in 2000. Kelly's first solo novel, *Planet of Whispers,* came out in 1984. It was followed by *Freedom Beach,* a mosaic novel written in collaboration with John Kessel, and then by the solo novels *Look Into the Sun and Wildside,* as well as the chapbook novella, *Burn*. His short work has been collected in *Think Like a Dinosaur* and *Strange But Not a Stranger*. His most recent book are a series of anthologies co-edited with John Kessel: *Feeling Very Strange: The Slipstream Anthology, The Secret History of Science Fiction, Digital Rapture: The Singularity Anthology, Rewired: The Post-Cyberpunk Anthology,* and *Nebula Awards Showcase 2012*. Born in Minneola, New York, Kelly now lives with his family in Nottingham, New Hampshire.

The Pure Product
JOHN KESSEL

I arrived in Kansas City at one o'clock on the afternoon of the thirteenth of August. A Tuesday. I was driving the beige 1983 Chevrolet Citation that I had stolen two days earlier in Pocatello, Idaho. The Kansas plates on the car I'd taken from a different car in a parking lot in Salt Lake City. Salt Lake City was founded by the Mormons, whose god tells them that in the future Jesus Christ will come again.

I drove through Kansas City with the windows open and the sun beating down through the windshield. The car had no air conditioning, and my shirt was stuck to my back from seven hours behind the wheel. Finally I found a hardware store, "Hector's" on Wornall. I pulled into the lot. The Citation's engine dieseled after I turned off the ignition; I pumped the accelerator once and it coughed and died. The heat was like syrup. The sun drove shadows deep into corners, left them flattened at the feet of the people on the sidewalk. It made the plate glass of the store window into a dark negative of the positive print that was Wornall Road. August.

The man behind the counter in the hardware store I took to be Hector himself. He looked like Hector, slain in vengeance beneath the walls of paintbrushes—the kind of semi-friendly, publicly optimistic man who would tell you about his crazy wife and his ten-penny nails. I bought a gallon of kerosene and a plastic paint funnel, put them into the trunk of the Citation, then walked down the block to the Mark Twain Bank. Mark Twain died at the age of seventy-five with a heart full of bitter accusations against the Calvinist god and no hope for the future of humanity. Inside the bank I went to one of the desks, at which sat a Nice Young Lady. I asked about starting a business checking account. She gave me a form to fill out, then sent me to the office of Mr. Graves.

Mr. Graves wielded a formidable handshake. "What can I do for you, Mr . . . ?"

"Tillotsen, Gerald Tillotsen," I said. Gerald Tillotsen, of Tacoma, Washington, died of diphtheria at the age of four weeks—on September 24, 1938. I have a copy of his birth certificate.

"I'm new to Kansas City. I'd like to open a business account here, and perhaps take out a loan. I trust this is a reputable bank? What's your exposure in Brazil?" I looked around the office as if Graves were hiding a woman behind the hat stand, then flashed him my most ingratiating smile.

Mr. Graves did his best. He tried smiling back, then looked as if he had decided to ignore my little joke. "We're very sound, Mr. Tillotsen."

I continued smiling.

"What kind of business do you own?"

"I'm in insurance. Mutual Assurance of Hartford. Our regional office is in Oklahoma City, and I'm setting up an agency here, at 103rd and State Line." Just off the interstate.

He examined the form. His absorption was too tempting.

"Maybe I can fix you up with a policy? You look like dead meat."

Graves' head snapped up, his mouth half-open. He closed it and watched me guardedly. The dullness of it all! How I tire. He was like some cow, like most of the rest of you in this silly age, unwilling to break the rules in order to take offense. "Did he really say that?" he was thinking. "Was that his idea of a joke? He looks normal enough." I did look normal, exactly like an insurance agent. I was the right kind of person, and I could do anything. If at times I grate, if at times I fall a little short of or go a little beyond convention, there is not one of you who can call me to account.

Graves was coming around. All business.

"Ah—yes, Mr. Tillotsen. If you'll wait a moment, I'm sure we can take care of this checking account. As for the loan—"

"Forget it."

That should have stopped him. He should have asked after my credentials, he should have done a dozen things. He looked at me, and I stared calmly back at him. And I knew that, looking into my honest blue eyes, he could not think of a thing.

"I'll just start the checking account with this money order," I said, reaching into my pocket. "That will be acceptable, won't it?"

"It will be fine," he said. He took the form and the order over to one of the secretaries while I sat at the desk. I lit a cigar and blew some smoke rings. I'd purchased the money order the day before in a post office in Denver. Thirty dollars. I didn't intend to use the account very long. Graves returned with my sample checks, shook hands earnestly, and wished me a good day. Have a *good* day, he said. I *will,* I said.

Outside, the heat was still stifling. I took off my sports coat. I was sweating so much I had to check my hair in the side view mirror of my car. I walked down the street to a liquor store and bought a bottle of chardonnay and a bottle of Chivas Regal. I got some paper cups from a nearby grocery. One final errand, then I could relax for a few hours.

In the shopping center that I had told Graves would be the location for my nonexistent insurance office, I had noticed a sporting goods store. It was about three o'clock when I parked in the lot and ambled into the shop. I looked at various golf clubs: irons, woods, even one set with fiberglass shafts. Finally I selected a set of eight Spalding irons with matching woods, a large bag, and several boxes of Top Flites. The salesman, who had been occupied with another customer at the rear of the store, hustled up, his eyes full of commission money. I gave him little time to think. The total cost was $612.32. I paid with a check drawn on my new account, cordially thanked the man, and had him carry all the equipment out to the trunk of the car.

I drove to a park near the bank; Loose Park, they called it. I felt loose. Cut loose, drifting free, like one of the kites people were flying that had broken its string and was ascending into the sun. Beneath the trees it was still hot, though the sunlight was reduced to a shuffling of light and shadow on the brown grass. Kids ran, jumped, swung on playground equipment. I uncorked my bottle of wine, filled one of the paper cups, and lay down beneath a tree, enjoying the children, watching young men and women walking along the footpaths.

A girl approached. She didn't look any older than seventeen. Short, slender, with clean blond hair cut to her shoulders. Her shorts were very tight. I watched her unabashedly; she saw me watching and left the path to come over to me. She stopped a few feet away, hands on her hips. "What are you looking at?" she asked.

"Your legs," I said. "Would you like some wine?"

"No thanks. My mother told me never to accept wine from strangers." She looked right through me.

"I take what I can get from strangers," I said. "Because I'm a stranger, too."

I guess she liked that. She was different. She sat down and we chatted for a while. There was something wrong about her imitation of a seventeen-year-old; I began to wonder whether hookers worked the park. She crossed her legs and her shorts got tighter. "Where are you from?" she asked.

"San Francisco. But I've just moved here to stay. I have a part interest in the sporting goods store at the Eastridge Plaza."

"You live near here?"

"On West Eighty-ninth." I had driven down Eighty-ninth on my way to the bank.

"I live on Eighty-ninth! We're neighbors."

It was exactly what one of my own might have said to test me. I took a drink of wine and changed the subject. "Would you like to visit San Francisco someday?"

She brushed her hair back behind one ear. She pursed her lips, showing off her fine cheekbones. "Have you got something going?" she asked, in queerly accented English.

"Excuse me?"

"I said, have you got something going?" she repeated, still with the accent—the accent of my own time.

I took another sip. "A bottle of wine," I replied in good mid-western 1980s.

She wasn't having any of it. "No artwork, please. I don't like artwork."

I had to laugh: my life was devoted to artwork. I had not met anyone real in a long time. At the beginning I hadn't wanted to, and in the ensuing years I had given up expecting it. If there's anything more boring than you people it's us people. But that was an old attitude. When she came to me in K.C., I was lonely and she was something new.

"Okay," I said. "It's not much, but you can come for the ride. Do you want to?"

She smiled and said yes.

As we walked to my car, she brushed her hip against my leg. I switched the bottle to my left hand and put my arm around her shoulders in a fatherly way. We got into the front seat, beneath the trees on a street at the edge of the park. It was quiet. I reached over, grabbed her hair at the nape of her neck, and jerked her face toward me, covering her little mouth with mine. Surprise: she threw her arms around my neck and slid across the seat into my lap. We did not talk. I yanked at the shorts; she thrust her hand into my pants. St. Augustine asked the Lord for chastity, but not right away.

At the end she slipped off me, calmly buttoned her blouse, brushed her hair back from her forehead. "How about a push?" she asked. She had a nail file out and was filing her index fingernail to a point.

I shook my head and looked at her. She resembled my grandmother. I had never run into my grandmother, but she had a hellish reputation. "No thanks. What's your name?"

"Call me Ruth." She scratched the inside of her left elbow with her nail. She leaned back in her seat, sighed deeply. Her eyes became a very bright, very hard blue.

While she was aloft I got out, opened the trunk, emptied the rest of the chardonnay into the gutter, and used the funnel to fill the bottle with kerosene. I plugged it with a kerosene-soaked rag. Afternoon was sliding into evening as I started the car and cruised down one of the residential streets. The houses were like those of any city or town of that era of the Midwest USA: white frame, forty or fifty years old, with large porches and small front yards. Dying elms hung over the street. Shadows stretched across the sidewalks. Ruth's nose wrinkled; she turned her face lazily toward me, saw the kerosene bottle, and smiled.

Ahead on the left-hand sidewalk I saw a man walking leisurely. He was an average sort of man, middle-aged, probably just returning from work, enjoying the quiet pause dusk was bringing to the hot day. It might have been Hector; it might have been Graves. It might have been any one of you. I punched the cigarette lighter, readied the bottle in my right hand, steering with my leg as the car moved slowly forward.

"Let me help," Ruth said. She reached out and steadied the wheel with her slender fingertips. The lighter popped out. I touched it to the rag; it smoldered and caught. Greasy smoke stung my eyes. By now the man had noticed us. I hung my arm, holding the bottle, out the window. As we passed him, I tossed the bottle at the sidewalk like a newsboy tossing a rolled-up newspaper. The rag flamed brighter as it whipped through the air; the bottle landed at his feet and exploded, dousing him with burning kerosene. I floored the accelerator; the motor coughed, then roared, the tires and Ruth both squealing in delight. I could see the flaming man in the rearview mirror as we sped away.

On the Great American Plains, the summer nights are not silent. The fields sing the summer songs of insects—not individual sounds, but a high-pitched drone of locusts, crickets, cicadas, small chirping things for which I have no names. You drive along the superhighway and that sound blends with the sound of wind rushing through your opened windows, hiding the thrum of the automobile, conveying the impression of incredible velocity. Wheels vibrate, tires beat against the pavement, the steering wheel shudders, alive in your hands, droning insects alive in your ears. Reflecting posts at the roadside leap from the darkness with metronomic regularity, glowing amber in the headlights, only to vanish abruptly into the ready night when you pass. You lose track of time, how long you have been on the road, where you are going. The fields scream in your ears like a thousand lost, mechanical souls, and you press your foot to the accelerator, hurrying away.

When we left Kansas City that evening we were indeed hurrying. Our direction was in one sense precise: Interstate 70, more or less due east, through Missouri in a dream. They might remember me in Kansas City, at the same time wondering who and why. Mr. Graves scans the morning paper over his grapefruit: MAN BURNED BY GASOLINE BOMB. The clerk wonders why he ever accepted an unverified counter check, without a name or address printed on it, for six hundred dollars. The check bounces. They discover it was a bottle of chardonnay. The story is pieced together. They would eventually figure out how—I wouldn't lie to myself about that (I never lie to myself)—but the why would always escape them. Organized crime, they would say. A plot that misfired.

Of course, they still might have caught me. The car became more of a liability the longer I held on to it. But Ruth, humming to herself, did not seem to care, and neither did I. You have to improvise those things; that's what gives them whatever interest they have.

Just shy of Columbia, Missouri, Ruth stopped humming and asked me, "Do you know why Helen Keller can't have any children?"

"No."

"Because she's dead."

I rolled up the window so I could hear her better. "That's pretty funny," I said.

"Yes. I overheard it in a restaurant." After a minute she asked, "Who's Helen Keller?"

"A dead woman." An insect splattered itself against the windshield. The lights of the oncoming cars glinted against the smear it left.

"She must be famous," said Ruth. "I like famous people. Have you met any? Was that man you burned famous?"

"Probably not. I don't care about famous people anymore." The last time I had anything to do, even peripherally, with anyone famous was when I changed the direction of the tape over the lock in the Watergate so Frank Wills would see it. Ruth did not look like the kind who would know about that. "I was there for the Kennedy assassination," I said, "but I had nothing to do with it."

"Who was Kennedy?"

That made me smile. "How long have you been here?" I pointed at her tiny purse. "That's all you've got with you?"

She slid across the seat and leaned her head against my shoulder. "I don't need anything else."

"No clothes?"

"I left them in Kansas City. We can get more."

"Sure," I said.

She opened the purse and took out a plastic Bayer aspirin case. From it she selected two blue-and-yellow caps. She shoved her palm up under my nose. "Serometh?"

"No thanks."

She put one of the caps back into the box and popped the other under her nose. She sighed and snuggled tighter against me. We had reached Columbia and I was hungry. When I pulled in at a McDonald's she ran across the lot into the shopping mall before I could stop her. I was a little nervous about the car and sat watching it as I ate (Big Mac, small Dr. Pepper). She did not come back. I crossed the lot to the mall, found a drugstore, and bought some cigars. When I strolled back to the car she was waiting for me, hopping from one foot to another and tugging at the door handle. Serometh makes you impatient. She was wearing a pair of shiny black pants, pink-and-white-checked sneakers, and a hot pink blouse.

" 's go!" she hissed.

I moved even slower. She looked like she was about to wet herself, biting her soft lower lip with a line of perfect white teeth. I dawdled over my keys. A security guard and a young man in a shirt and tie hurried out of the mall entrance and scanned the lot. "Nice outfit," I said. "Must have cost you something."

She looked over her shoulder, saw the security guard, who saw her. "Hey!" he called, running toward us. I slid into the car, opened the passenger door. Ruth had snapped open her purse and pulled out a small gun. I grabbed her arm and yanked her into the car; she squawked and her shot went wide. The guard fell down anyway, scared shitless. For the second time that day I tested the Citation's acceleration; Ruth's door slammed shut and we were gone.

"You scut," she said as we hit the entrance ramp of the interstate. "You're a scut-pumping Conservative. You made me miss." But she was smiling, running her hand up the inside of my thigh. I could tell she hadn't ever had so much fun in the twentieth century.

For some reason I was shaking. "Give me one of those seromeths," I said.

Around midnight we stopped in St. Louis at a Holiday Inn. We registered as Mr. and Mrs. Gerald Bruno (an old acquaintance) and paid in advance. No one remarked on the apparent difference in our ages. So discreet. I bought a copy of the *Post-Dispatch*, and we went to the room. Ruth flopped down on the bed, looking bored, but thanks to her gunplay I had a few more things to take care of. I poured myself a glass of Chivas, went into the bathroom, removed the toupee and flushed it down the toilet, showered, put a new blade in my old razor, and shaved the rest of the hair from my head. The Lex Luthor look. I cut my scalp. That got me laughing, and I could not stop. Ruth peeked through the doorway to find me dabbing the crown of my head with a bloody Kleenex.

"You're a wreck," she said.

I almost fell off the toilet laughing. She was absolutely right. Between giggles I managed to say, "You must not stay anywhere too long, if you're as careless as you were tonight."

She shrugged. "I bet I've been at it longer than you." She stripped and got into the shower. I got into bed.

The room enfolded me in its gold-carpet green-bedspread mediocrity. Sometimes it's hard to remember that things were ever different. In 1596 I rode to court with Essex; I slept in a chamber of supreme garishness (gilt escutcheons in the corners of the ceiling, pink cupids romping on the walls), in a bed warmed by any of the trollops of the city I might want. And there in the Holiday Inn I sat with my drink, in my pastel blue pajama bottoms, reading a late-twentieth-century newspaper, smoking a cigar. An earthquake in Peru estimated to have killed eight thousand in Lima alone. Nope. A steel worker in Gary, Indiana, discovered to be the murderer of six prepubescent children, bodies found buried in his basement. Perhaps. The president refuses to enforce the ruling of his Supreme Court because it "subverts the will of the American people." Probably not.

We are everywhere. But not everywhere.

Ruth came out of the bathroom, saw me, did a double take. "You look—perfect!" she said. She slid in the bed beside me, naked, and sniffed at my glass of Chivas. Her lip curled. She looked over my shoulder at the paper. "You can understand that stuff?"

"Don't kid me. Reading is a survival skill. You couldn't last here without it."

"Wrong."

I drained the scotch. Took a puff on the cigar. Dropped the paper to the floor beside the bed. I looked her over. Even relaxed, the muscles in her arms and along the tops of her thighs were well defined.

"You even smell like one of them," she said.

"How did you get the clothes past their store security? They have those beeper tags clipped to them."

"Easy. I tried on the shoes and walked out when they weren't looking. In the second store I took the pants into a dressing room, cut the alarm tag out of the waistband, and put them on. I held the alarm tag that was clipped to the blouse in my armpit and walked out of that store, too. I put the blouse on in the mall women's room."

"If you can't read, how did you know which was the women's room?"

"There's a picture on the door."

I felt tired and old. Ruth moved close. She rubbed her foot up my leg, drawing the pajama leg up with it. Her thigh slid across my groin. I started to get hard. "Cut it out," I said. She licked my nipple.

I could not stand it. I got off the bed. "I don't like you."

She looked at me with true innocence. "I don't like you, either."

Although he was repulsed by the human body, Jonathan Swift was passionately in love with a woman named Esther Johnson. "What you did at the mall was stupid," I said. "You would have killed that guard."

"Which would have made us even for the day."

"Kansas City was different."

"We should ask the cops there what they think."

"You don't understand. That had some grace to it. But what you did was inelegant. Worst of all it was not gratuitous. You stole those clothes for yourself, and I hate that." I was shaking.

"Who made all these laws?"

"I did."

She looked at me with amazement. "You're not just a Conservative. You've gone native!"

I wanted her so much I ached. "No I haven't," I said, but even to me my voice sounded frightened.

Ruth got out of the bed. She glided over, reached one hand around to the small of my back, pulled herself close. She looked up at me with a face that held nothing but avidity. "You can do whatever you want," she whispered. With a feeling that I was losing everything, I kissed her. You don't need to know what happened then.

I woke when she displaced herself: there was a sound like the sweep of an arm across fabric, a stirring of air to fill the place where she had been. I looked around the still brightly lit room. It was not yet morning. The chain was across the door; her clothes lay on the dresser. She had left the aspirin box beside my bottle of scotch.

She was gone. Good, I thought, now I can go on. But I found that I couldn't sleep, could not keep from thinking. Ruth must be very good at that, or perhaps her thought is a different kind of thought from mine. I got out of the bed, resolved to try again but still fearing the inevitable. I filled the tub with hot water. I got in, breathing heavily. I took the blade from my razor. Holding my arm just beneath the surface of the water, hesitating only a moment, I cut deeply one, two, three times along the veins in my left wrist. The shock was still there, as great as ever. With blood streaming from me I cut the right wrist. Quickly, smoothly. My heart beat fast and light, the blood flowed frighteningly; already the water was stained. I felt faint—yes—it was going to work this time, yes. My vision began to fade—but in the last moments before consciousness fell away I saw, with sick despair, the futile wounds closing themselves once again, as they had so many times before. For in the future the practice of medicine may progress to the point where men need have little fear of death.

The dawn's rosy fingers found me still unconscious. I came to myself about eleven, my head throbbing, so weak I could hardly rise from the cold bloody water. There were no scars. I stumbled into the other room and washed down one of Ruth's megamphetamines with two fingers of scotch. I felt better immediately. It's funny how that works sometimes, isn't it? The maid knocked as I was cleaning the bathroom. I shouted for her to come back later, finished as quickly as possible, and left the hotel immediately. I ate Shredded Wheat with milk and strawberries for breakfast. I was full of ideas. A phone book gave me the location of a likely country club.

The Oak Hill Country Club of Florissant, Missouri, is not a spectacularly wealthy institution, or at least it does not give that impression. I'll bet you that the membership is not as purely white as the stucco clubhouse. That was all right with me. I parked the Citation in the mostly empty parking lot, hauled my new equipment from the trunk, and set off for the locker room, trying hard to look like a dentist. I successfully ran the gauntlet of the pro shop, where the proprietor was telling a bored caddy why the Cardinals would fade in the stretch. I could hear running water from the showers as I shuffled into the locker room and slung the bag into a corner. Someone was singing the "Ode to Joy," abominably.

I began to rifle through the lockers, hoping to find an open one with someone's clothes in it. I would take the keys from my benefactor's pocket and proceed along my merry way. Ruth would have accused me of self-interest; there was a moment in which I accused myself. Such hesitation is the seed of failure: as I paused before a locker containing a likely set of clothes, another golfer entered the room along with the locker-room attendant. I immediately began undressing, lowering my head so that the locker door hid my face. The golfer was soon gone, but the attendant sat down and began to leaf through a worn copy of *Penthouse*. I could come up with no better plan than to strip and enter the showers. Amphetamine daze. Perhaps the kid would develop a hard-on and go to the john to take care of it.

There was only one other man in the shower, the symphonic soloist, a somewhat portly gentleman who mercifully shut up as soon as I entered. He worked hard at ignoring me. I ignored him in return: *alle Menschen werden Brüder.* I waited a long five minutes after he left; two more men came into the showers, and I walked out with what composure I could muster. The locker-room boy was stacking towels on a table. I fished a five from my jacket in the locker and walked up behind him. Casually I took a towel.

"Son, get me a pack of Marlboros, will you?"

He took the money and left.

In the second locker I found a pair of pants that contained the keys to some sort of Audi. I was not choosy. Dressed in record time, I left the new clubs beside the rifled locker. My note read, "The pure products of America go crazy." There were three eligible cars in the lot, two 4000s and a Fox. The key would not open the door of the Fox. I was jumpy, but almost home free, coming around the front of a big Chrysler . . .

"Hey!"

My knee gave way and I ran into the fender of the car. The keys slipped out of my hand and skittered across the hood to the ground, jingling. Grimacing, I hopped toward them, plucked them up, glancing over my shoulder at my pursuer as I stooped. It was the locker-room attendant.

"Your cigarettes." He looked at me the way a sixteen-year-old looks at his father; that is, with bored skepticism. All our gods in the end become pitiful. It was time for me to be abruptly courteous. As it was, he would remember me too well.

"Thanks," I said. I limped over, put the pack into my shirt pocket. He started to go, but I couldn't help myself. "What about my change?"

Oh, such an insolent silence! I wonder what you told them when they asked you about me, boy. He handed over the money. I tipped him a quarter, gave him a piece of Mr. Graves' professional smile. He studied me. I turned and inserted the key into the lock of the Audi. A fifty-percent chance. Had I been the praying kind I might have prayed to one of those pitiful gods. The key turned without resistance; the door opened. The kid slouched back toward the clubhouse, pissed at me and his lackey's job. Or perhaps he found it in his heart to smile. Laughter—the Best Medicine.

A bit of a racing shift, then back to Interstate 70. My hip twinged all the way across Illinois.

I had originally intended to work my way east to Buffalo, New York, but after the Oak Hill business I wanted to cut it short. If I stayed on the interstate I was sure to get caught; I had been lucky to get as far as I had. Just outside of Indianapolis I turned onto Route 37 north to Fort Wayne and Detroit.

I was not, however, entirely cowed. Twenty-five years in one time had given me the right instincts, and with the coming of the evening and the friendly insects to sing me along, the boredom of the road became a new recklessness. Hadn't I already been seen by too many people in those twenty-five years? Thousands had looked into my honest face—and where were they? Ruth had reminded me that I was not stuck here. I would soon make an end to this latest adventure one way or another, and once I had done so, there would be no reason in God's green world to suspect me.

And so: north of Fort Wayne, on Highway 6 east, a deserted country road (what was he doing there?), I pulled over to pick up a young hitchhiker. He wore a battered black leather jacket. His hair was short on the sides, stuck up in spikes on top, hung over his collar in back; one side was carrot-orange, the other brown with a white streak. His sign, pinned to a knapsack, said "?" He threw the pack into the backseat and climbed into the front.

"Thanks for picking me up." He did not sound like he meant it.

"Where you going?"

"Flint. How about you?"

"Flint's as good as anywhere."

"Suit yourself." We got up to speed. I was completely calm. "You should fasten your seat belt," I said.

"Why?"

The surly type. "It's not just a good idea. It's the law."

He ignored me. He pulled a crossword puzzle book and a pencil from his jacket pocket. "How about turning on the light?"

I flicked on the dome light for him. "I like to see a young man improve himself," I said.

His look was an almost audible sigh. "What's a five-letter word for 'the lowest point'?"

"Nadir," I replied.

"That's right. How about 'widespread'; four letters?"

"Rife."

"You're pretty good." He stared at the crossword for a minute, then rolled down his window and threw the book, and the pencil, out of the car. He rolled up the window and stared at his reflection in it. I couldn't let him get off that easily. I turned off the interior light, and the darkness leapt inside.

"What's your name, son? What are you so mad about?"

"Milo. Look, are you queer? If you are, it doesn't matter to me but it will cost you . . . if you want to do anything about it."

I smiled and adjusted the rearview mirror so I could watch him—and he could watch me. "No, I'm not queer. The name's Loki." I extended my right hand, keeping my eyes on the road.

He looked at the hand. "Loki?"

As good a name as any. "Yes. Same as the Norse god."

He laughed. "Sure, Loki. Anything you like. Fuck you."

Such a musical voice. "Now there you go. Seems to me, Milo—if you don't mind my giving you my unsolicited opinion—that you have something of an attitude problem." I punched the cigarette lighter, reached back and pulled a cigar from my jacket on the backseat, in the process weaving the car all over Highway 6. I bit the end off the cigar and spat it out the window, stoked it up. My insects wailed. I cannot explain to you how good I felt.

"Take, for instance, this crossword puzzle book. Why did you throw it out the window?"

I could see Milo watching me in the mirror, wondering whether he should take me seriously. The headlights fanned out ahead of us, the white lines at the center of the road pulsing by like a rapid heartbeat. Take a chance, Milo. What have you got to lose?

"I was pissed," he said. "It's a waste of time. I don't care about stupid games."

"Exactly. It's just a game, a way to pass the time. Nobody ever really learns anything from a crossword puzzle. Corporation lawyers don't get their Porsches by building their word power with crosswords, right?"

"I don't care about Porsches."

"Neither do I, Milo. I drive an Audi."

Milo sighed.

"I know, Milo. That's not the point. The point is that it's all a game, crosswords or corporate law. Some people devote their lives to Jesus; some devote their lives to artwork. It all comes to pretty much the same thing. You get old. You die."

"Tell me something I don't already know."

"Why do you think I picked you up, Milo? I saw your question mark and it spoke to me. You probably think I'm some pervert out to take advantage of you. I have a funny name. I don't talk like your average middle-aged businessman. Forget about that." The old excitement was upon me; I was talking louder and louder, leaning on the accelerator. The car sped along. "I think you're as troubled by the materialism and cant of life in America as I am. Young people like you, with orange hair, are trying to find some values in a world that offers them nothing but crap for ideas. But too many of you are turning to extremes in response. Drugs, violence, religious fanaticism, hedonism. Some, like you I suspect, to suicide. Don't do it, Milo. Your life is too valuable." The speedometer touched eighty, eighty-five. Milo fumbled for his seat belt but couldn't find it.

I waved my hand, holding the cigar, at him. "What's the matter, Milo? Can't find the belt?" Ninety now. A pickup went by us going the other way, the wind of its passing beating at my head and shoulder. Ninety-five.

"Think, Milo! If you're upset with the present, with your parents and the schools, think about the future. What will the future be like if this trend toward valuelessness continues in the next hundred years? Think of the impact of the new technologies! Gene splicing, gerontology, artificial intelligence, space exploration, biological weapons, nuclear proliferation! All accelerating this process! Think of the violent reactionary movements that could arise—are arising already, Milo, as we speak—from people's desire to find something to hold on to. Paint yourself a picture, *Milo,* of the kind of man or woman another hundred years of this process might produce!"

"What are you talking about?" He was terrified.

"I'm talking about the survival of values in America! Simply that." Cigar smoke swirled in front of the dashboard lights, and my voice had reached a shout. Milo was gripping the sides of his seat. The speedometer read 105. "And you, *Milo,* are at the heart of this process! If people continue to think the way you do, *Milo,* throwing their crossword puzzle books out the windows of their Audis all across America, the future will be full of absolutely valueless people! Right, MILO?" I leaned over, taking my eyes off the road, and blew smoke into his face, screaming, "ARE YOU LISTENING, MILO? MARK MY WORDS!"

"Y-yes."

"GOO, GOO, GA-GA-GAA!"

I put my foot all the way to the floor. The wind howled through the window, the gray highway flew beneath us,

"Mark my words, Milo," I whispered. He never heard me. "Twenty-five across. Eight letters. N-i-h-i-l—"

My pulse roared in my ears, there joining the drowned choir of the fields and the roar of the engine. Body slimy with sweat, fingers clenched through the cigar, fists clamped on the wheel, smoke stinging my eyes. I slammed on the brakes, downshifting immediately, sending the transmission into a painful whine as the car slewed and skidded off the pavement, clipping a reflecting marker and throwing Milo against the windshield. The car stopped with a jerk in the gravel at the side of the road, just shy of a sign announcing, WELCOME TO OHIO.

There were no other lights on the road, I shut off my own and sat behind the wheel, trembling, the night air cool on my skin. The insects wailed. The boy was slumped against the dashboard. There was a star fracture in the glass above his head, and warm blood came away on my fingers when I touched his hair. I got out of the car, circled around to the passenger's side, and dragged him from the seat into the field adjoining the road. He was surprisingly light. I left him there, in a field of Ohio soybeans on the evening of a summer's day.

The city of Detroit was founded by the French adventurer Antoine de la Mothe, sieur de Cadillac, a supporter of Comte de Pontchartrain, minister of state to the Sun King, Louis XIV. All of these men worshiped the Roman Catholic god, protected their political positions, and let the future go hang. Cadillac, after whom an American automobile was named, was seeking a favorable location to advance his own economic interests. He came ashore on July 24, 1701, with fifty soldiers, an equal number of settlers, and about one hundred friendly Indians near the present site of the Veterans Memorial Building, within easy walking distance of the Greyhound Bus Terminal.

The car did not run well after the accident, developing a reluctance to go into fourth, but I didn't care. The encounter with Milo had gone exactly as such things should go, and was especially pleasing because it had been totally unplanned. An accident—no order, one would guess—but exactly as if I had laid it all out beforehand. I came into Detroit late at night via Route 12, which eventually turned into Michigan Avenue. The air was hot and sticky. I remember driving past the Cadillac plant; multitudes of red, yellow, and green lights glinting off dull masonry and the smell of auto exhaust along the city streets. I found the sort of neighborhood I wanted not far from Tiger Stadium: pawnshops, an all-night deli, laundromats, dimly lit bars with red Stroh's signs in the windows. Men on street corners walked casually from noplace to noplace.

I parked on a side street just around the corner from a 7-Eleven. I left the motor running. In the store I dawdled over a magazine rack until at last I heard the racing of an engine and saw the Audi flash by the window. I bought a copy of *Time* and caught a downtown bus at the corner. At the Greyhound station I purchased a ticket for the next bus to Toronto and sat reading my magazine until departure time.

We got onto the bus. Across the river we stopped at customs and got off again. "Name?" they asked me.

"Gerald Spotsworth."

"Place of birth?"

"Calgary." I gave them my credentials. The passport photo showed me with hair. They looked me over. They let me go.

I work in the library of the University of Toronto. I am well-read, a student of history, a solid Canadian citizen. There I lead a sedentary life. The subways are clean, the people are friendly, the restaurants are excellent. The sky is blue. The cat is on the mat.

We got back on the bus. There were few other passengers, and most of them were soon asleep; the only light in the darkened interior was that which shone above my head. I was very tired, but I did not want to sleep. Then I remembered that I had Ruth's pills in my jacket pocket. I smiled, thinking of the customs people. All that was left in the box were a couple of tiny pink tabs. I did not know what they were, but I broke one down the middle with my fingernail and took it anyway. It perked me up immediately. Everything I could see seemed sharply defined. The dark green plastic of the seats. The rubber mat in the aisle. My fingernails. All details were separate and distinct, all interdependent. I must have been focused on the threads in the weave of my pants leg for ten minutes when I was surprised by someone sitting down next to me. It was Ruth. "You're back!" I exclaimed.

"We're all back," she said. I looked around and it was true: on the opposite side of the aisle, two seats ahead, Milo sat watching me over his shoulder, a trickle of blood running down his forehead. One corner of his mouth pulled tighter in a rueful smile. Mr. Graves came back from the front seat and shook my hand. I saw the fat singer from the country club, still naked. The locker-room boy. A flickering light from the back of the bus: when I turned around there stood the burning man, his eye sockets two dark hollows behind the wavering flames. The shopping-mall guard. Hector from the hardware store. They all looked at me.

"What are you doing here?" I asked Ruth.

"We couldn't let you go on thinking like you do. You act like I'm some monster. I'm just a person."

"A rather nice-looking young lady," Graves added.

"People are monsters," I said.

"Like you, huh?" Ruth said. "But they can be saints, too."

That made me laugh. "Don't feed me platitudes. You can't even read."

"You make such a big deal out of reading. Yeah, well, times change. I get along fine, don't I?"

The mall guard broke in. "Actually, miss, the reason we caught on to you is that someone saw you walk into the men's room." He looked embarrassed.

"But you didn't catch me, did you?" Ruth snapped back. She turned to me. "You're afraid of change. No wonder you live back here."

"This is all in my imagination," I said. "It's because of your drugs."

"It is all in your imagination," the burning man repeated. His voice was a whisper. "What you see in the future is what you are able to see. You have no faith in God or your fellow man."

"He's right," said Ruth.

"Bull. Psychobabble."

"Speaking of babble," Milo said, "I figured out where you got that goo-goo-goo stuff. Talk—"

"Never mind that," Ruth broke in. "Here's the truth. The future is just a place. The people there are just people. They live differently. So what? People make what they want of the world. You can't escape human failings by running into the past." She rested her hand on my leg. "I'll tell you what you'll find when you get to Toronto," she said. "Another city full of human beings."

This was crazy. I knew it was crazy. I knew it was all unreal, but somehow I was getting more and more afraid. "So the future is just the present writ large," I said bitterly. "More bull."

"You tell her, pal," the locker-room boy said.

Hector, who had been listening quietly, broke in. "For a man from the future, you talk a lot like a native."

"You're the king of bullshit, man," Milo said. " 'Some people devote themselves to artwork'! Jesus!"

I felt dizzy. "Scut down, Milo. That means 'Fuck you too.' " I shook my head to try to make them go away. That was a mistake: the bus began to pitch like a sailboat. I grabbed for Ruth's arm but missed. "Who's driving this thing?" I asked, trying to get out of the seat.

"Don't worry," said Graves. "He knows what he's doing."

"He's brain-dead," Milo said.

"You couldn't do any better," said Ruth, pulling me back down.

"No one is driving," said the burning man.

"We'll crash!" I was so dizzy now that I could hardly keep from being sick. I closed my eyes and swallowed. That seemed to help. A long time passed; eventually I must have fallen asleep.

When I woke it was late morning and we were entering the city, cruising down Eglinton Avenue. The bus had a driver after all—a slender black man with neatly trimmed sideburns who wore his uniform hat at a rakish angle. A sign above the windshield said, YOUR DRIVER—SAFE, COURTEOUS, and below that, on the slide-in nameplate, WILBERT CAUL. I felt like I was coming out of a nightmare. I felt happy. I stretched some of the knots out of my back. A young soldier seated across the aisle from me looked my way; I smiled, and he returned it briefly.

"You were mumbling to yourself in your sleep last night," he said.

"Sorry. Sometimes I have bad dreams."

"It's okay. I do too, sometimes." He had a round open face, an apologetic grin. He was twenty, maybe. Who knew where his dreams came from? We chatted until the bus reached the station; he shook my hand and said he was pleased to meet me. He called me "sir."

I was not due back at the library until Monday, so I walked over to Yonge Street. The stores were busy, the tourists were out in droves, the adult theaters were doing a brisk business. Policemen in sharply creased trousers, white gloves, sauntered along among the pedestrians. It was a bright, cloudless day, but the breeze coming up the street from the lake was cool. I stood on the sidewalk outside one of the strip joints and watched the videotaped come-on over the closed circuit. The Princess Laya. Sondra Nieve, the Human Operator. Technology replaces the traditional barker, but the bodies are more or less the same. The persistence of your faith in sex and machines is evidence of your capacity to hope.

Francis Bacon, in his masterwork *The New Atlantis,* foresaw the utopian world that would arise through the application of experimental science to social problems. Bacon, however, could not solve the problems of his own time and was eventually accused of accepting bribes, fined £40,000, and imprisoned in the Tower of London. He made no appeal to God, but instead applied himself to the development of the virtues of patience and acceptance. Eventually he was freed. Soon after, on a freezing day in late March, we were driving near Highgate when I suggested to him that cold might delay the process of decay. He was excited by the idea. On impulse he stopped the carriage, purchased a hen, wrung its neck, and stuffed it with snow. He eagerly looked forward to the results of his experiment. Unfortunately, in haggling with the street vendor he had exposed himself thoroughly to the cold and was seized by a chill that rapidly led to pneumonia, of which he died on April 9, 1626.

There's no way to predict these things.

When the videotape started repeating itself I got bored, crossed the street, and lost myself in the crowd.

First published in *Isaac Asimov's Science Fiction Magazine,* March 1986.

ABOUT THE AUTHOR

Born in Buffalo, New York, **John Kessel** now lives in Raleigh, North Carolina, where he is a professor of American Literature and the director of the Creative Writing program at North Carolina State University. Kessel made his first sale in 1975. His first solo novel, *Good News From Outer Space,* was released in 1988 to wide critical acclaim, but before that he had made his mark on the genre primarily as a writer of highly-imaginative, finely-crafted short stories, many of which have were assembled in his collection *Meeting in Infinity.* He won a Nebula Award in 1983 for his novella "Another Orphan," which was also a Hugo finalist that year, and has been released as an individual book. His story "Buffalo" won the Theodore Sturgeon Award in 1991, and his novella "Stories for Men" won the prestigious James Tiptree Jr. Memorial Award in 2003. His other books include the novel *Freedom Beach,* written in collaboration with James Patrick Kelly, and an anthology of stories from the famous Sycamore Hill Writers Workshop (which he also helps to run), called *Intersections,* co-edited by Mark L. Van Name and Richard Butner. His most recent books are a major novel, *Corrupting Dr. Nice,* and a two new collections, *The Pure Product* and *The Collected Kessel,* as well as a series of anthologies co-edited with James Patrick Kelly: *Feeling Very Strange: The Slipstream Anthology, The Secret History of Science Fiction, Digital Rapture: The Singularity Anthology, Rewired: The Post-Cyberpunk Anthology,* and *Nebula Awards Showcase 2012.*

Druids Reconstructed
LEE BEAVINGTON

Stonehenge rises like a crown above the horizon, ancient four-tonne bluestones fixed in a sacramental circle. The cryptic monument's sudden appearance through the windshield is seductive. Alone with these noble rocks, one's mind turns to ritual and rite, and druids. From Merlin and Terry Brooks to World of Warcraft and the neo-druids celebrating solstice at Stonehenge, the druid mythology ignites our imagination. Thirty thousand people in the USA identify themselves as druids, yet they bear little resemblance to the barbarian philosophers, as the Greeks called them, who purportedly set living men on fire. Caesar plainly describes ritual murder and human sacrifice as druidic practice. And what link, if any, do they have with Stonehenge?

History

Imagine a white-robed figure brandishing mistletoe while a great bull is prepped for sacrifice. This learned priesthood revered the elements, lived in sacred groves of oak and hazel, and presided over religious ceremonies. A dominant force in the Celtic world, druids once held rank and prestige across Western Europe. Diverse claims by historians suggest they were scientists, magicians, judges and kingmakers.

Caesar gave a Roman slant on druidism: guardians of ancient customs and animism, practitioners of divining, and reincarnation. The vast druidic lore took upwards of twenty years to study in completion, according to Caesar.

The fog of time shrouds the druids in mystery. The earliest record of the name *druidae* dates back to second century BCE, in a work by Greek historian Sotion of Alexandria. The word *druid* holds dual meaning: oak, true, and solid derives from the Greek *druidēs,* while the Old Celtic term *druídecht* means magic. Nature and wisdom.

Druids have become mythologized by both 17th century scholars and 20th century romanticists. Finding authentic druid lore—not interpretations or artifacts of uncertain origin—is like studying all religions in search of the one true faith. Most surviving texts offer subjective analysis.

History erased the druid's chapter, as not a single piece of their oral tradition has survived. Celtic fragments found in excavations and various texts offer brief glimpses of habit and ritual, but few sources support other independent accounts. The word druid (in Celtic, Greek or Latin form) is not found in any pre-Christian inscription. Therefore, any connection of druids to monuments or sculptures requires some level of conjecture. Grave archaeology, ceremonial sites, and Romano-Celtic art depicting ritual practices—such as The Wicker Image in *Britannia Antiqua Illustrata*—only allow for radiocarbon dating and tentative inferences. The official suppression by Roman authority two thousand years ago helped convert druidic history to an idealized mythology.

Ceremonial Practice

Pliny the Elder offers the only complete depiction of druidic ceremonial practice. During a time of fasting, brookweed and flowering *Selago* were gathered in meticulous fashion. Six days after the full moon, two massive bulls, muscles rippling beneath their white skin, were prepared for sacrifice. The rite started with a white-robed druid who is said to use a golden sickle (more likely gilded bronze) to cut a hearty mistletoe stem from an oak, and the sacrifice commenced.

In Norse mythology, mistletoe could kill a god, as Balder, the son of Odin, was slain by an arrow of mistletoe. Pliny suggests druids used this parasitic plant to cure animal infertility. Mistletoe fruit ripens around winter solstice, a time of birth and renewal, and symbolizes immortality. Modern ecology places mistletoe as a keystone species, as studies show a positive relationship between its presence and animal diversity. Perhaps the druids understood mistletoe's ecological benefits.

The Gundestrup cauldron, from 1st century BCE, offers further insight into druidic customs. This gilded silver vessel was found in the Raevemosen Bog in Jutland, Denmark, and is covered in mythic narrative art, likely of Celtic origin. An army stands in full war gear surrounding a sacred tree. Deer, snake, horse, dog, and elephant are inscribed—the latter suggests Asian origin, but Celtic coins also bore images of elephants. Bull and human sacrifice are both depicted; many texts indicate druids led sacrificial ceremonies. However, the Gundestrup cauldron's history is steeped in supposition.

Sacrificial rituals were employed to appease the gods and help combat enemies, disease or drought. "Then finally they kill the victims, praying to God to render his gift propitious to those on whom he has bestowed it." (Pliny, *Natural History* XVI, 95.) Some druids, according to Caesar, vowed to immolate themselves. He goes on to describe "wicker-work images of vast size, the limbs of which they fill with living men and set on fire."

> It is judged that the punishment of those who participated in theft or brigandage or other crimes are more pleasing to the immortal gods; but when the supplies of this kind fail, they even go so low as to inflict punishment on the innocent. (Caesar, *Gallic Wars* VI, 13.)

Strabo, a Greek historian, wrote, "they would strike a man who had been consecrated for sacrifice in the back with a sword, and make prophecies based on his death-spasms." (Strabo, *Geography* IV, 4, 5.) Yet Strabo, like Caesar, simply reiterated the Posidonian texts, often without acknowledging this source. Posidonius, a Greek philosopher, is one of the few historians who likely encountered druids during his travels through Gaul (the territories of Western Europe where Celtic

Gauls lived). Others, such as the 1st century Roman historian Tacitus, wrote that British druids "deemed it indeed a duty to cover their altars with the blood of captives and to consult their deities through human entrails." (Tacitus, *Annals* XIV, 30-31.) Of the limited early texts, enough mention animal and human sacrifice to suggest druids engaged in such rituals.

Truth versus Fiction

A portrait of a white-clad druid atop the large branch of an oak, with sickle in hand, has influenced druidic perception to this day. The illustration's origin is unknown, yet clearly inspired by Pliny the Elder's account. A bull is portrayed with its horns bound, while pottery plates, jugs, and a basket suggest preparation for a feast. Both Welsh Druids and neo-druids (present-day druids that venerate nature) include elements of Pliny's account—and this illustration—in their mandates. Thus one image of ambiguous origin has thrust potential misconceptions hundreds of years forward to the present.

Julius Caesar presents the most detailed report on the druid's role in society. Book VI of *Commentarii de Bello Gallico* explains their exemption from taxes and military service, status equitable to nobles, and their role as guardians of tradition and purveyors of judgement. " ... they hold various lectures and discussions on astronomy, on the extent and geographical distribution of the globe, [and] on the different branches of natural philosophy." Druids follow the Pythagorean philosophy, where "the soul does not die and that after death it passes from one body into another."

After the start of the Common Era in the Gregorian calendar, a closer examination of the texts reveals a marked shift in opinion. Druids began to be perceived with loathing and contempt. Romans perpetuated their uncouth savagery, and referred to their wicked religion as barbarous and inhuman. Pliny even hints at ritual cannibalism. This shift coincides with a change in Gaulish society from a monarchy to a magistrate, and a decline in druid stature. The hostile manner in which Caesar, Strabo and others chronicled the druids was likely in response to an active rebellion against Rome. To counter this resistance, Roman historians portrayed paganism in sinister terms.

The druids *did* exist, but their traditions and beliefs cannot be confirmed. Unsubstantiated claims put William Blake as an Archdruid, as he frequently referred to them in his *Prophetic Books,* which included illustrations of Stonehenge and Avebury. Other literati, such as Thomas Grey and William Wordsmith, identified themselves with the ancient priesthood. But these were part of a much later revival, starting with

John Aubrey's writings in the late 1600s, and the genesis in 1781 of the *Ancient Order of Druids*.

Diviciacus, a Gaul chieftain, is perhaps history's only recorded druid. Caesar described him as a soldier and statesman, while Cicero, one of Rome's pre-eminent philosophers and orators, labelled him not only a druid but a scholar of natural phenomena with the ability to foretell the future through divination and inference. He did this through the study of bird flight, an idea Tacitus rejected as superstition. Cicero claims to have discussed philosophy with Diviciacus. (Cicero, *De Divinatione* I, 90.)

Decline of Druidism

How did the druids, once the elite of Gaulish society, fall into obscurity? The Romans welcomed Celtic gods into their Pantheon, but forbade pagan worship. Caesar perpetuated the druidic ritual of human sacrifice in order to gain public support for his war in Gaul. In Britain, Suetonius Paulinus led the attack on Anglesey, purportedly the last druid stronghold, as recorded by Tacitus:

> ... a circle of Druids, lifting their hands to heaven and showering imprecations, struck the troops with such an awe at the extraordinary spectacle that, as though their limbs were paralysed, they exposed their bodies to wounds without an attempt at movement. Then, reassured by their general, and inciting each other never to flinch before ... fanatics, they charged behind the standards, cut down all who met them, and enveloped the enemy in his own flames.
> (Tacitus, *Annals* XIV, 30-31.)

Rome prevailed. In early British literature, the word druid became obsolete. However, the druids of Scotland and Ireland were left unscathed by Roman aggression.

The Stonehenge Connection

Walter Pope wrote *The Salisbury Ballad* in 1676:

> I will not forget these Stones that are set
>   In a round, on *Salsbury* Plains
> Tho' who brought 'em there, 'tis hard to declare,
>   The Romans, or Merlin, or Danes

Pope does not mention pagan priests. Inigo Jones, a noted 17th century English architect, discards the druidic connection to Stonehenge on the basis that classical sources contain no reference to druid or Briton possessing architectural aptitude. But then, as a whole, druid references are scarce in any tradition. Jones considered Stonehenge Roman, as detailed in his posthumously published *The most notable Antiquity of Great Britain, vulgarly called Stone-heng* (sic). Some credit Danes as the architects of Stonehenge, based on superficial similarities with Danish megalithic monuments.

Neo-druids celebrate solstice within Stonehenge's two concentric circles. The huge bluestones are believed to have come from the Preseli Hills of west Wales, over two hundred and fifty kilometers away, transported either by the Irish Sea Glacier or via a human transport mechanism not yet fathomed by modern scholars. Bluestone is a generic term; in reality, Stonehenge is comprised of at least twenty different types of rock. The word trilithon (Greek for "possessing three stones") refers to the arrangement of two tall, vertical slabs with a third placed horizontally on top.

Stonehenge's multi-phase construction lasted one hundred and fifty years, with four-tonne stones being erected about 2500 BCE. In the first phase, a circular ditch and bank measuring one hundred and ten meters across was built. Flint tools and deer and oxen bones have been excavated from this trench, fire and beast suggesting a druid connection. Yet the druid-Stonehenge correlation is based on speculation; several other theories present equally plausible hypotheses.

Recent discoveries by the Stonehenge Riverside Project help explain Stonehenge's purpose. Ancient human remains, put at 3,000 BCE by radiocarbon dating, suggest these giant sandstone blocks were erected about five hundred years *after* the site was first used as a burial ground. Cremations were dug from what are called the Aubrey Holes, meaning pre-Stonehenge served as a cemetery. Around two hundred and forty people were buried beneath Stonehenge over the course of five hundred years, selected for this sacred site perhaps because of special status, or membership to an elite dynasty of rulers.

Modern Stonehenge is owned by English Heritage, which was granted an exclusion zone in 1985. Cloak and staff-bearing neo-druids clash with police over usage rights in incidents such as the Battle of the Beanfield, where police in riot gear chased away travellers hoping to celebrate summer solstice near Stonehenge. Each year, the number of pagan pilgrims increases. If no claim of ownership can be substantiated, how did druids become firmly cemented with Stonehenge?

The medieval period sparked little interest in druids. In the latter half of the 17th century, John Aubrey drew on the works of Caesar and—along with his own systematic archaeological fieldwork in Wiltshire—assigned druidic origin to Stonehenge, the first to make this connection. He argued Stonehenge and Avebury were pre-Roman temples, and therefore druidic, the dominant priesthood at the time, an idea now embedded in English folklore.

Evolving Mythology

Historians over the last few centuries have transformed druids into virtuous sages, their barbarianism and sacrificial rituals conveniently eschewed. The pendulum of druidism could not have shifted further out on both sides. First, exaggeration by historians to help justify the war in Gaul, followed thousands of years later by a denial of savage cruelty on the part of the druids.

The initial awe of seeing these bluestones rise from a time before Buddha or Christ sours upon closer examination of the henge. Some stones are missing, others fallen, reconstructed in the early 1900s to stand once more. But what truly spoil the mystery are the bustling tourists flashing their cameras, the self-guiding headphones strapped to their ears, and the perfunctory gift shop.

Today, accurate accounts of the druids have all but vanished. Encounter diluted to report, and report faded into rumour. The *Historia Brittonum*—a medieval publication whose author remains suitably anonymous—elucidates the Stonehenge riddle best: "at what time this was done, or by what people, or for what memorial or significance, is unknown." Despite the scarcity of facts, and the lack of a single written word attributed to their sacred order, the druid myth endures.

For a moment, let us put aside the pre-recorded audio, the tacky Stonehenge trinkets, and the pieced together fragments of philosophers. Go back to that first day the stones were erected, and every trilithon stood impossibly high. Under the midnight sky, step quietly around these megaliths into moon shadow. Touch the glacier-sent bluestone with a hand that helped construct this marvel of human creativity, long before machine, at a time when the abacus served as our latest technology. Let your tongue taste the shifting winds across the plains during the intersection of the seasons. Pause inside the meticulous circle of concentric stone, your feet planted on the center of this celestial map, a place that invites the spirits of mistletoe and bull. Come to understand how human and plant, earth and stone, and the gods of the sky are all interwoven. Perhaps, then, you are one step closer to understanding the extraordinary enigma that is the druid.

Select Bibliography

- Caesar, Julius. *Commentarii de Bello Gallico.*
- Cicero. *De Divinatione.*
- Green, Miranda J. *The World of the Druids,* Thames and Hudson, 1997.
- Milius, Susan. "Mistletoe, of All Things, Helps Juniper Trees." *Science News* 161.1, January 2002.
- Owen, James. "Stonehenge Was Cemetery First and Foremost, Study Says," *National Geographic News,* May 29, 2008.
- Piggott, Stuart. *The Druids,* Thames and Hudson, 1975.
- Pliny the Elder. *Natural History.*
- Sammes, Aylett. *Britannia Antiqua Illustrata,* 1676.
- Squire, Charles. *Celtic Myth and Legend,* Newcastle Publishing, 1975.
- Stonehenge Riverside Project (www.sheffield.ac.uk/archaeology/research/2.4329/index).
- Tacitus. *Annals.*

ABOUT THE AUTHOR

Lee Beavington is an award-winning author of fiction, nonfiction and poetry. His novella, "Evolution's End," appears in *Writers of the Future XXII,* and his book *Common Plants of Greater Vancouver* is a required textbook for both science and arts students. In addition to teaching ecology, cell biology and genetics in the biology lab at Kwantlen University, he also served as primary photography for three of Lone Pine's nature books, including Wild Berries of British Columbia. His Master's thesis explores the intersection of creative process, nature experience, storytelling and transformational change.

A Craftsman of No Small Skill:
A Conversation with David Drake

JEREMY L. C. JONES

I first met David Drake a little over ten years ago. At the time, I'd read more of his science fiction than his fantasy; I preferred his Hammers Slammers and military SF to his Republic of Cinnabar Navy (RCN) series and other space opera fiction.

What I'd read had moved me deeply and answered many questions I'd had about my grandfather's and my father's experiences in the military. I've long admired Drake's ability to talk and write openly about his experiences in Vietnam and Cambodia and to reveal the horrors of war through powerful storytelling—to shed light on the unlightable darkness.

If more of our combat veterans could write with clarity and effectiveness, maybe—just maybe—there'd be fewer wars.

Over the years, I've continued to gravitate toward his grimmer fiction, with a special fondness for the stories in *Grimmer than Hell* and the novel *Redliners,* and for the oddball novel-in-stories and homage to Manly Wade Wellman, *Old Nathan.*

But, honestly, I love all his books. These books go past mere entertainment for me. They move me. They get under my skin. They become a part of me.

Drake and I have spoken and corresponded, on and off the record, since we first met and we've agreed to disagree on one fundamental point. I believe that he is an important science fiction and fantasy writer—and important *writer,* regardless of genre. He doesn't.

It is not false modesty.

"I think I am a first-rate craftsman," said Drake, "and that is not a small thing. My dad was a first-rate electrician. His father was possibly the best sheet-metal smith in the United States. I'm a craftsman also and I am damn proud of it, but nobody's ever heard of my father or my grandfather and there's no particular reason they should've heard of me. But I'm proud of the craft."

Below, Drake and I talk about the craft and the work. We talk about plotting, plodding, and language. He opts for lean prose and weighty ideas.

Language shouldn't be there to show what a fine writer the storyteller is, according to Drake. Language shouldn't clothe ideas is fancy garb. Language should, as Drake says below, describe a scene "clearly and simply to the reader."

In the 70s and 80s, Drake took "show and don't tell" to heart and was, as he put it, "pilloried by the critics as being pro-war because I didn't *say* I was anti-war. I described things that any sane person would find horrific. God knows, *I* found them horrific. But I didn't say so. Of course, I opposed these things. Any idiot would know that. But, of course, they didn't."

It's hard to imagine anyone reading a pro-war agenda into Drake's fiction, but part of the power of well-crafted fiction is, I suppose, that it invites multiple interpretations.

As a follow-up to a visit to Drake's home this past summer, we spoke on the telephone this fall. I caught him "trying to get into plotting the next one" and he wasn't "there yet." The "next one" was the fourth and final book in the Books of the Elements series for Tor. "Plotting" will ultimately result in a 10- or 15,000 words plot outline.

Is it hard to go from summarizing what happens to dramatizing what happens?

No. I had dinner years ago with Stephen King and I mentioned how I plotted. He looked at me and said, "Don't you get really bored when you're writing it?" I said, "No." But obviously, he would've. [Laughing] Obviously, his way works, too. His way works for him.

What's holding you up with this one?

I'm just starting it. It always takes me a couple of months to get started. It's an exhausting job to write a novel and when I finish I am just totally wrung out. Mentally, I want to dive right into the next novel, but frankly I can't. I don't know that anybody could. Oh, that's not true. Some people definitely could. But I'm not them.

Right now I am reading the *Dionysiaca of Nonnos,* the conquest of India. I'm gathering. I'm jotting down little bits. I've gone through a book of Indian folklore. I'm going over past notes and excerpting. It's just a matter of getting a mass of stuff. I know where this one is going, but with 150,000 words, there's a lot of business and it's just a matter of getting that business down.

So when you say you're "trying to get into plotting the next one," it's more about recovering from the previous one, than something unique about this one.

Yeah. It's always like this. There's nothing particularly difficult about this one. I did a novelette after I finished the previous novel but that doesn't really count. That was sort of a break. Now I am trying to focus on the novel.

I did the third of the Elements series, then I did the plot outline for the second of the Hinterlands series that John [Lambshead] is writing called *Into the Maelstrom*—he's working on that now—then I did the next RCN novel. You know, bang, bang, without a lot of rest. It was really pretty hard doing the RCN novel like that. It was just a lot of work. But, you know, that's what they pay me for.

I don't especially like to do plot outlines for other people, but in this case I'd done the *Into the Hinterlands* outline quite a long time ago, mid-90s, I guess, and [the contracted writer] didn't get around to writing it, so Toni [Weisskopf] wound up giving it to John Lambshead to execute and she was pleased with the result, but [laughing] that meant that I had to plot the other two novels in the series. I'm not planning to do more plot outlines for other people but I do have one more to do for John just because it's sort of grandfathered in.

I wonder if going from RCN, which is filled with characters that you've spent years with, to this fourth book in a series which is, intellectually, one of your most challenging—

I keep trying to push.

You come off an uphill climb and now you're at an even steeper climb—straight up a cliff. What've you gotten yourself into, here?

The thing is, it's all volunteer. And that's an important thing. Nobody is doing this to me. If it fails, I screwed up. And that's okay. I mean, I'm okay with the thought that if I screw up and fail, I should fail. That pushes me to try and do it right. Now, I don't need a lot of push in that direction. But my friend Mark [Van Name] pointed out something to me years ago—he pointed out that when I did *Northworld,* it really tore me apart. I was having back spasms so serious just out of tension that my left leg was numb for a few weeks after I'd gotten the book done. I was really doing something new. He said, "Now you're doing the Isles series. Each of those books is more complex than *Northworld* was and you just take it in stride." I thought about that, and yeah, you do, you learn new stuff *by doing it.*

I think I'm probably best known for my action writing and I certainly try to do good action and I think I do good action. But I have a history and Latin background and I graduated from a first class law school. If I didn't like intellectual puzzles, I wouldn't have that background.

It almost seems like you have two identities with the two different publishers. There's the Baen writer—science fiction, action—and the Tor writer—fantasy, more intellectual—and those two writers aren't always thought of as being the same person.

I am writing very simple, clear, direct prose. No matter what I am writing. That's not the perception of me, certainly not in Fantasy but even in SF. I like to think that all my work is done at a high intellectual level, because it's no fun if it isn't. That doesn't mean I have to show people that I am smart. The work ought to do that. I don't need to throw in long words. Because I know long words. I don't have to throw in Latin because I know Latin. As a matter of fact, I make a point of always translating any Latin that I'm using.

The simplicity of the language goes straight to the ideas. The ideas are not simple, not easily digested, which may contribute to the . . . complexity of the perception of your work. It's not easy to say what your work is or what your work isn't, because you've tapped into the truth and the truth is not easily simplified. It is complicated. Show me a simple sentence in a Hammer's Slammers short story and it will probably tell me something that I can't discuss simply.

[Laughing] Probably tell you something you didn't want to know. People shouldn't read a book and say, "This is beautifully written." They ought to say, "Wow, was that a story!" Same thing with a speech, by the way. This is something I was taught long, long ago in speech class. If people leave the auditorium saying, "Oh, that was a wonderful speech," you've failed. You want them to say, "By God, we've got to do something about this problem!" It's a whole different thing. Critics will be more positively impressed by fine language than they will be by simple language that communicates thoughts. They will. It's just a reality.

You've said before that what Baen Books does well is find and publish *stories*, and that a good story is a good story. But, uh . . . what makes a good story?

A good story has a beginning, a middle, and an end. Honestly, that implies an arc that implies things are happening and that's as close as I can come to it. My friend Mark says, arguing that Baen focuses on story—he says that there isn't an editor in the business who will say, "I'm not interested in story" or even "I'm not *primarily* interested in a *good* story." Baen Books isn't different in that way, but the result is different. I think in many cases if you come out of a literary background you will focus on literary values—language, vocabulary, complexity of sentence structure—all of which are marks of fine writing and fine writing is seriously the enemy describing a scene clearly and simply to the reader and I really think it's important to if you're telling a story to tell it in a simple direct fashion rather than to worry abut the beauty of your prose. I'm not against beautiful prose. But clarity of expression is a mark of good storytelling.

Backing up, once you have the plot outline, how does your life change for the next how many ever months?

I get up in the morning. I read the portion I did yesterday and make quick edits on it. This is partially reading myself into the process. Then I sit with the outline beside me and I write the next portion. I have it broken out into scenes in the outline and I write the next scene. Some days I finish a scene or start a scene or sometimes it feels like I've been battering on this forever and it may be five days before I finish the damn scene. That's usually because it's long and because it's difficult for some reason that doesn't involve the work itself. It's where my head is and other stuff going on and all that.

Mark has said that once I get started I'm just a machine and that's kind of true and I want it to be that way. I've done all the hard part. I've got all the cute little bits. Sure, I break scenes up, I change stuff, and I move stuff around. Going from 15,000 words to 150,000 words obviously there's a lot of addition going on, but it's mechanical. The writing can be a slog.

Do you ever just put a title at the top of the page and go.

I used to do it all the time in the 60s and 70s. And I didn't finish stories. I tried it with novels. I spent 12 years after I sold my first story trying to write a novel. And I couldn't. I'd poop out. I'd get into the middle of it and I'd be convinced it was crap and I wouldn't finish it. Nowadays when I'm in the middle of a novel, I'm convinced it's crap but I finish it, because it's just a matter of plodding forward and I want to hang myself and I'm convinced that "I was able to do this before but I've completely just lost it and they'd be better off reading the phone book" but I keep on going. I'm very depressed, but you know, frankly, on a good day I'm pretty depressed anyway [laughing].

So there's a lot of sunshine in this process?

There are various ways of dealing with the situation [of writing a novel], but any one that works for you is okay . . . My way works for me. I haven't hanged myself thus far.

Is the plotting part linear?

The first portion of it is to gather a huge amount of data, not infrequently saying, "This will work!" When I say that, I'm not really sure where it will work or how it will work but "oh, that's a good bit, I need to use that" and when I get a huge amount of data then I start putting it together into either a plot outline or a series of individual sequences; that is, if I have multiple viewpoints and I generally do if I'm writing a long novel. I may start out trying to run a sequence of one character, one viewpoint, and then do another or I may try to do a chapter from all two or four viewpoints or a combination of these. It tends to be slightly different every time which puzzles me. I'm not consciously doing it in different fashions but it always is and I don't know what that means.

Is there a visual element. Do you map or draw things out?

In the sense you mean, I'll choreograph battles and I'll choreograph dinner tables. I need to know where all these people are sitting.

But I will also have a picture of an 18th century dining room beside me or a picture of this hotel in Boise, Idaho in front of me. I have lots and lots of things with pictures in them and I'll think, "I want something of this sort of tone," and I'll grab a volume out and start paging through until I find "oh, that'll do for it" or "this isn't what I was thinking of, but I can use it very well for this purpose and it will make it different in this fashion."

You do a good bit of writing outdoors, too, don't you?

All of it. I do my work on two laptops and then I save my work to a base unit, which is a desktop. Then I'll call it up for the next burst. I sit in different places according to what the weather is and where the sun is. Either I want to be in the sun or out of the sun. I am never in exactly the same place at any two periods of work.

Was the Northworld series the last of the landmark, stressful books?

Nothing else has been as physically stressful. There was one I did—*ARC Riders*—which was a collaboration but I wrote, I think, all but six sections. It was the editor's idea and she thought it would be a good idea to start this alternate history book in a world in which the Vietnam

War hadn't ended. I said, "Okay, I can do that." And I could do it. It made me very, very, very depressed. And I decided I would never go directly back—that wasn't really direct, but you know what I mean—into Vietnam, again.

There were also the Tom Kelly books, *Skyripper* and *Fortress*. Those were an idea of Tom Doherty's. They were stressful in a different way because there is a lot of similarity between me and the viewpoint character Tom Kelly. That's me on a really bad day, the mindset. The hell of it is, it's a way I could've gone and I didn't. By great determination, I did not go that way. He's a man who's really consumed with anger, and I'm not that man but I wasn't making it up either and I think that was difficult for the people around me and I would not have done another one except Tom really, really pushed me for one. He said later when I sent him the intro for the combined edition, *Loose Cannon*, "Gee, Dave, if I'd known you hated it that much I wouldn't have made you do it." [Laughing] I said, "Tom, I told you I didn't want to do it!"

That's one of those cases where I'm staying calm and people aren't listening to what I'm saying they're listening to how I'm saying it. Oh, well!

Two things with those books: they very directly approach things that are difficult to deal with—Vietnam and your anger there was someone else involved in the conception of the idea. Those two things say, "Move out, Dave's going to be difficult to live with."

[Laughing] He was. But I'm a saintly human being now. [More laughter.]

No college writing colleges or MFA programs for you, eh?

It's a completely different mindset. It's fine for the people who want it, but it isn't what I wanted. Some of them it's worked out well for. I think in some cases it's been very seriously damaging. [A science fiction writer] can be taught to loathe the thing he does well [in a workshop].

I wonder, when you write non-fiction about Vietnam, is that as stressful?

No. I've always told the truth. As the years go on, I'm even more willing to tell the truth. I've never lied. I wasn't any kind of hero, and I've never claimed that. Considered clinically, nothing happened to me.

Then Mark [Van Name] sat me down and said, "Did you see this? Did this happen to you? Did you do this?" "Yeah. Yeah. Yeah." Mark said, "You realize any of the things I just mentioned would be five years of therapy for a civilian."

Stories you told me ten years ago about your experiences in Vietnam still haunt me, and I'm very removed from them.

Be glad.

So, I guess there's no point in even asking if you'd want to write a mainstream novel with no fantastical elements.

Not only "no," but "hell no." I write what I do for a reason. And it's not because I'm too dumb to figure out there's another thing to do.

ABOUT THE AUTHOR

Jeremy L. C. Jones is a freelance writer, editor, and teacher. He is the Staff Interviewer for *Clarkesworld Magazine* and a frequent contributor to *Kobold Quarterly* and *Booklifenow.com*. He teaches at Wofford College and Montessori Academy in Spartanburg, SC. He is also the director of Shared Worlds, a creative writing and world-building camp for teenagers that he and Jeff VanderMeer designed in 2006. Jones lives in Upstate South Carolina with his wife, daughter, and flying poodle.

Another Word:
Two and a Half Writers
DANIEL ABRAHAM

My attitude toward pseudonyms has always been a little idiosyncratic. I started off using them as a way to tell readers what kind of book to expect. Daniel Abraham? He writes third-person epic fantasy. MLN Hanover? First-person urban fantasy, complete with the tramp stamp tattoo and complicated love life. James SA Corey (of whom I am the James half, Ty Franck being the Corey)? Third-person space opera.

The idea was—and is—that someone who really loved Daniel Abraham's Long Price Quartet books would probably be put off and disappointed picking up a book and discovering it's urban fantasy. My various names aren't a secret. There's tabs for each of them there at the top of the website. I talk about them in public (just like this). I adopted pseudonyms not as a way to disguise myself, but as a courtesy for the readers.

And it turns out that taking on new names does some other very interesting things. In the six years since I broke out MLN Hanover as my first fake identity, the publishing strategy has turned into a kind of unintentional experiment about the publishing business, celebrity, identity, and reputation. By being MLN Hanover and James SA Corey, I've found out some things about what it is to be Daniel Abraham too.

The first real surprise I had with the pseudonyms came with MLN. Even though I didn't keep the fact of my identity secret, it came as a surprise to a lot of people that Daniel Abraham and MLN Hanover were the same person. My career as a writer didn't really take off before the Internet became the central fact of American (and increasingly world) culture.

With blogs and social media, there's a sense that everything is known, or at least is available to be known with pretty minimal effort. I had the sense—wrongly—that by simply not keeping something secret, it would become common knowledge. In practice, it was weirder than that, and I still have people who are shocked and surprised to discover what I cop to often and in public. The feeling of intimacy and connection that the Internet gives me is exaggerated, and this was my first unintentional proof of that. What I say in public isn't a secret, but it also isn't known. We are all of us so inundated and overwhelmed with information that what seems like it should be common knowledge about me among those who bother to care still isn't. Everything about my public personas is always at least partly introduction, and I think, always will be.

The other thing about MLN was that I started writing urban fantasy at a time when the common wisdom was that UF was written and read mostly by women. In choosing the name, I took the classical route of obscuring my gender with initials. Given the context—a "women's" genre, a first-person female protagonist, an ungendered name—a lot of folks assumed the author of The Black Sun's Daughter books was a woman, and that's an impression I was comfortable with people having. In fact, I got lot of letters from readers who said that they wouldn't have picked the books up if they'd known I was a man. Generally, they were letters from folks who liked the books, but not always.

It's also served as a springboard for conversations about persona, gender and race. I'm certainly not the only male urban fantasy writer who obscured his gender with an ambiguous name. T. A. (Tim) Pratt, comes to mind. The practice is, I understand, even more common in the more "women's"- identified genre of romance. And there is a long tradition of women hiding their gender with pseudonyms for equally market driven reasons. I don't feel uncomfortable writing under MLN Hanover and being mistaken for a woman. I find the fact that there are spaces within publishing (and also within our wider shared culture) in which being female is a kind of locally privileged position at the same time that the larger context remains powerfully misogynistic fascinating. On the other hand, I wouldn't in a million years write as Raj Avasarala or Gustavo Martinez even if the market became very rewarding of Indian or Latino identities. It isn't a question I considered deeply before I became MLN Hanover. It is one I think about now.

Another thing that having three names showed me—and continues to show me—is how important it is to not have all my professional eggs in one basket. I know a lot of professional writers, and of the people I know making a living at this trade, everyone who's been at it more than four or five years has had their careers shot out from under them at least once. For me, the first time came when my first publisher, Tor, decided to drop the Long Price Quartet books. The fourth one had just come out in hardback, I had the proposal in to my editor for a new series called The Dagger and the Coin, and the news came in that not only were they passing on the new series, but they'd decided not to release the fourth Long Price book in paperback. It was devastating, but it would have been more devastating if MLN Hanover's first book hadn't been on the Barnes & Noble trade paperback bestsellers list. For months, it looked like Daniel Abraham's career was done, until Orbit—previously my UK publisher—decided to let me take another swing with their US house. The reason I wasn't a total mess for those long, terrible weeks was that even as I watched my career founder and die, it wasn't my only career. I had a backup, which because it carried a different name on the cover, wasn't related in the computers to my epic fantasies. I didn't set out to build a firewall between my books, but I'd done it anyway. Daniel Abraham's sales numbers didn't hurt MLN Hanover, and so I, as both of them, got to keep right on paying my bills through the storm.

James SA Corey came later, and what I learned from having that name in the mix is to my mind, the most interesting—and important—insight that my unintentional experiment in names has given me. Thanks to the team at Orbit and an agent who is nothing short of amazing, Daniel Abraham has been having a resurgence in the last few years. The Dagger and the Coin books have sold fairly well, and in a lot of foreign markets to boot. MLN Hanover has struggled. Though the reviews of each successive book have been better and better, the sales numbers haven't grown. James SA Corey, though? Those books caught lightning in a jar. The first of them, *Leviathan Wakes*, is in its ninth US printing. It's been picked up in 20 countries around the world. The guys who wrote the first Iron Man movie have teamed up with the woman who developed *Breaking Bad*, and they're looking to turn it into a television series (more strength to their arms). My first appearance on *The New York Times* bestsellers list was as James SA Corey.

But here's the thing: I'm not suddenly a better writer when I'm working with Ty on the Expanse books. I'm not suddenly a worse writer when I'm doing urban fantasy. Daniel Abraham's books didn't stop being good at the end of the Long Price Quartet and get better with The Dagger and the Coin series. I have three careers going right now, and each of them is performing differently in the stores. There are reasons for all of that, but the one reason that doesn't apply is *me*. That's the real gift James SA Corey and MLN Hanover have given me. Every time I look at my Bookscan numbers, I can see that the books sell or don't, the series build or don't, based on factors that aren't the author. I cannot imagine how hard it would have been for me to watch Daniel Abraham's career run aground without MLN there to hold me up. Or what it would be like to watch MLN's numbers falter without Daniel Abraham and James SA Corey to remind me that commercial success isn't just about my name. Careers fall down all the time, and it's rarely about the skill of the writer.

My imaginary selves have taught me that my sense of being in the center of things, and being well connected to people is an illusion. That my alternate identities have boundaries that I haven't wholly understood. They have protected me from the worst professional downturns, and given me enough emotional distance from my sales numbers that the success of failure of any particular project can stay with that project instead of defining who I am.

Not bad for folks who don't even exist.

ABOUT THE AUTHOR

Daniel Abraham is a writer of genre fiction with a dozen books in print and over thirty published short stories. His work has been nominated for the Nebula, World Fantasy, and Hugo Awards and has been awarded the International Horror Guild Award. He also writes as MLN Hanover and (with Ty Franck) as James S. A. Corey. He lives in the American Southwest.

Editor's Desk:
Behind the Scenes Tour
NEIL CLARKE

Last month, I provided the numbers behind *Clarkesworld,* but numbers alone don't give you the whole story of what it takes to produce this magazine. As promised, this month I will not only reveal some of what goes on behind the scenes but who is responsible for each issue.

Original Fiction

As mentioned in my previous editorial, we receive seven to eight hundred short story submissions per month. The first pass through these stories is conducted by the ever amazing slush readers, (Cynthia Bermudez, John Emery DeLong, Terra Lemay, Aimee Picchi) and me. I'm reading approximately 40-50% of those stories and the slush readers comment on the rest. Stories are then rejected or moved onto the next round.

Sean Wallace and I handle the next round. A story doesn't get published unless we both agree on it. While we have similar taste, I'm more likely to be the "no" vote. This process typically whittles the pile down to between two and five stories. Additionally, a few stories throughout the year are via invitation. In the past his happened with much greater frequency.

Once we've decided to purchase a story, I send out acceptance letters and contracts. The next stage involves editing the story (the amount of which varies wildly), layout, and initial proofreading.

Reprint Fiction

Since April, Gardner Dozois has been responsible for the selection of each month's reprints. We have some basic guidelines for the age and length of the stories he can choose, but otherwise, the only other criteria he has is that the story isn't currently available in another magazine or the author's website. (I don't like to step on the heels of other publications. I just don't find it polite.) After we've verified that the stories meet our criteria, Gardner contacts the author and, if they are interested, contracts the story. The story, contract, author bio, and photo are then passed to me for layout and proofreading.

Non-Fiction

Kate Baker is our non-fiction editor. Each month, she receives a number of pitches or solicits opinion pieces from potential contributors. If the query sounds like a good fit for *Clarkesworld,* she'll request a finished copy of the article and make a final decision. Additionally, Daniel Abraham completes a unique Another Word column every other month with the gaps filled by other invited industry professionals. Approved projects are then contracted and the editing process commences. When the lead article or Another Word opinion column is complete, Kate sends the completed works, contracts, bios, and photos to me for layout and proofreading. Together, Kate and I also work on fine-tuning my editorial each month.

Our interviews are usually handled by Jeremy L. C. Jones, typically in consultation with me and later edited by Kate.

Podcasts

In addition to her non-fiction responsibilities, Kate Baker narrates, hosts, and produces each episode of our podcast. Five times per month, she closes the door to her TARDIS recording booth and records for forty-five minutes to an hour depending on the length of the story. She spends another two or three hours on each file, editing out all the mistakes and spaces within the recording, adds some original music, and sends me a file to preview. I then add the finished product to our website and push into our distribution channels.

Art

Every month, I spend hours searching through a wide variety of online art sites and portfolios that artists have sent along. When I locate a suitable piece, I do a quick search to make sure it hasn't been previously used as cover art and then contact the artist to see of the rights are available. Quite often rights are already reserved for a game or book, so this process can be quite time-consuming. If the rights are available and the artist interested, I'll send them a contract and start mocking up the cover in InDesign.

Production

I'm responsible for the web, ebook, print, and subscription files for each issue. Most of the content received from authors and other contributors is delivered in Word format. I use a program called Dreamweaver to create the html files for the website and load them into our system.

From there, I have home-grown programs to convert the HTML and various indexes to the EPUB and Amazon subscription feed formats. (The final 5% of the work is done by hand.) The EPUB files are then converted to MOBI—for standalone Kindle ebooks—and RTF—for import into InDesign to make our print edition PDFs. The InDesign files are then restyled and converted to PDF for submission to the company that produces our iPad and Android apps.

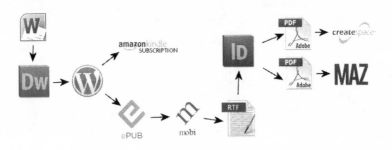

Podcast episodes are added to our website as they become available. Links to individual podcast episodes are then manually dropped into the apps.

Finances

I've saved the boring part of the business for me. I manage the books, issue payments (via check or PayPal), and track the income from ebooks, subscriptions, print editions, donations, advertising, and anything else we come up with. And of course, there's the taxes . . .

And that ends our tour. The gift shop is down the hall. Have a happy holiday season and an amazing new year!

ABOUT THE AUTHOR ──────────────────────────

Neil Clarke is the editor of *Clarkesworld Magazine*, owner of Wyrm Publishing and a 2013 Hugo Nominee for Best Editor (short form). He currently lives in NJ with his wife and two children.

About the Artist
JULIE DILLON

Julie Dillon is a freelance illustrator working in Northern California. She creates science fiction and fantasy artwork for books, magazines and games. Julie is a 2013 Hugo Award Nominee for Best Artist.

WEBSITE

www.jdillon.net

Made in the USA
Columbia, SC
19 September 2018